BRAVE BOY

A Perfect Boys Novel

K.M. Neuhold

CONTENTS

Title Page
Blurb   1
Copyright   3
Chapter 1   4
Chapter 2   18
Chapter 3   28
Chapter 4   35
Chapter 5   47
Chapter 6   65
Chapter 7   77
Chapter 8   105
Chapter 9   113
Chapter 10   124
Chapter 11   137
Chapter 12   148
Chapter 13   163
Chapter 14   178

Chapter 15	200
Chapter 16	218
Chapter 17	231
Chapter 18	239
Chapter 19	254
Chapter 20	275
Chapter 21	284
Chapter 22	293
Epilogue	302
About the Author	308

BLURB

As long as LonelyDaddy is on the other side of the computer screen, there's a chance he could be the man Emerson has been dreaming of.

I've gotten used to being alone, to disappearing inside the fictional worlds between the pages of a book and letting my lonely life fade away.

Books have never judged me for the stutter I can't control. Books have never abandoned me. Books have never let me down. Then again, books have never hugged me or told me they loved me either, so my plan is far from perfect.

The first time I lay eyes on the tall, red-haired Kiernan with a beard for days and shoulders made for scratch marks, I wanted to crawl onto his lap and call him Daddy. The only problem is, I can never seem to string two words together around him... Heck, I'd be happy to manage to get even one word out, like maybe "yes," preferably over and over again.

I thought making an online dating profile would be the hardest part, but it turns out getting up the courage to meet the man I've been messaging is even more difficult. Could LonelyDaddy be Kiernan? And if he is, is there any chance he'll want to keep me? Can I be his brave boy?

***Brave Boy is the online love-sweet, ginger Daddy—totally swoony—second book in the Perfect Boys series and can be read as a stand-alone.

COPYRIGHT

Brave Boy© 2021 by K.M.Neuhold

All rights reserved. No part of this book may be used or reproduced in any manner whatsoever without written permission except in the case of brief quotations embodied in critical articles or reviews.

This book is a work of fiction. Names, characters, businesses, organizations, places, events and incidents either are the product of the author's imagination or are used fictitiously. Any resemblance to actual persons, living or dead, events, or locales is entirely coincidental.

Book and Cover design by Natasha Snow Designs
Cover Image by CJC Photography
Cover Model Brock Grady
Editor: Editing by Rebecca
Proof Reading by Abbie Nicole

CHAPTER 1

Emerson

I tug my favorite T-shirt—purple with a sparkly unicorn on the front—over my head and then drag my fingers through my wild curls in a half-hearted attempt to tame them. Glancing down at myself, I fiddle with the hem of my shirt and blow out a long breath, wondering…just, *wondering*.

That's the thing about being invited to a surprise party for your best friend's Daddy— and I *don't* mean *father*—it makes a guy wonder certain things, like whether he'll ever find the firm but gentle Daddy of his own dreams or if he's better off giving up and settling for his head full of fantasies instead.

It isn't that I'm not cute enough to be the boy some perfect Daddy lusts after. I'm not tragically oblivious to my own good looks or anything. I fully own my slim-but-toned figure, bouncy booty, and bow-shaped pink lips. I see the way men of all ages and types look at me. The problem comes when I open my mouth.

My phone vibrates on my dresser, dancing over the messy surface while I hurry to pull up my jeans and then answer it before I miss the call.

"Hey, S-S-SSS-Sterling."

"Em, I'm so glad ya answered. You already on the way over?" I smile to myself at the sound of my friend's accent. I've never told him, but I think it's really cute. I'm sure his Daddy, Barrett, tells him all the time. A small jealous pang twists in my chest.

"No," I say, checking my reflection once more before sitting on the foot of my bed so I can put my shoes on.

"Perfect. Can I ask you to do me a teeny little favor? With all the planning I've been doin' all day, I forgot to pick up Daddy's cake. Ya couldn't stop by the bakery for me, could ya?"

"S-s-sss…" I huff out an annoyed breath at the way the word gets stuck on my lips. "Yes," I manage instead. "I'll l-leave now and be there s-s-soon."

"Thank you, thank you, thank you. I owe you big time. It's already paid for. You just have to swing by Hershman's and pick it up."

"You got it," I assure him again. If I'm honest, I'm relieved to have a task. I never got around to figuring out what kind of a present to take for a man who's a literal billionaire with everything he could possibly want. Doing a favor on the day of the party counts as a present, right?

I pause one more time to do a last check in the full-length hallway mirror. I'm not usually this vain, but it's not every night that I know I'm going to be bumping into a certain ginger-haired, wet-dream-inspiring, seriously-that-voice-though Daddy. At least I *think* Kiernan is a Daddy. From the conversations I've overheard between Barrett and his business partners, it seems they all are.

Not that it matters. I definitely *didn't* pick my favorite unicorn shirt in the hope that he'll give me that teasing smirk and say "cute shirt" like he did the first time we met. Of course, I immediately turned tomato red and forgot how to string two words together, so not the best first impression on my part. And it hasn't gotten much better since then. Every time I see him, I swear I somehow get even more tongue-tied than the last time. Hot mess: table for one.

Satisfied that I'm as cute as I'm going to manage, I grab my keys and head out the door.

Even with the stop at the bakery on the way, it's not long before I'm pulling into the massive driveway that leads up to Barrett's mansion. I shouldn't be surprised that a valet is waiting to take my keys when I climb out of my car.

I'm careful not to jostle the cake too much as I make my way up the large set of steps that lead to the front door. The cake is decorated with what appears to be fireflies made out of frosting and the words "Happy Birthday, Barrett." I don't want to be the cause of any tragically smeared frosting.

Sterling pulls open the door before I even make it all the way up the steps as if he's been waiting for me on the other side since we got off the phone. There's a distinct possibility that's exactly what he's been doing.

"You're a lifesaver," he says, relief written all over his face as he takes the cake from me and leads me inside.

"It's n-no p-p-problem," I assure him, glancing around as soon as we're inside for any sign that Kiernan is already here. Sterling heads straight for the kitchen with the cake, and I follow him.

"We have cake," he announces happily as we step into the large room with vaulted ceilings and marble countertops. Seems like a lot to worry about keeping clean if you ask me, but what do I know?

The kitchen is filled with people. I've met some of them before. Lorna, Barrett's sister; Nolan and Gannon, employees of his; and Alden, his other—and much more intimidating—business partner, are all here. And then there are some people I don't recognize. But no Kiernan.

I do my best to ignore the momentary flair of disappointment. I'm sad Kiernan isn't here because now I won't have the chance to blush and stutter like an idiot in his general direction? What an epic tragedy. *Eyeroll.*

"Em, so glad to see you!" Nolan greets me with a surprising amount of enthusiasm. He's the event planner for Russell Investments. Basically, it's his job to throw fabulous parties that encourage other rich people to fork over their money to good causes and business startups. He looks every bit the part, too, with glitter on his cheeks and a bright-pink, tailored tux. "Sterling and I were just discussing how things are going with your mobile library project, and I was telling him that I would love to get involved in whatever capacity would be helpful."

He takes a sip from the martini glass he's holding and smiles at me expectantly. I share a quick look with Sterling, wondering if he feels as thrown off by Nolan's earnest zeal as I am. He seems like a nice enough guy, but there's just something a little...overeager about him that I'm not sure how to handle.

"C-cool," I say with a smile, casting a quick look around in search of where I might get a drink of my own.

I spot what appears to be a makeshift bar and shuffle over to it, Nolan staying right at my side. "You know, I actually have some ideas I wanted to run by both of you about the libraries."

I nod along while I mix a drink, practicing the words in my head to tell him that they're really Sterling's thing; I'm just helping out. It always helps when I've practiced something ahead of time, but it's no guarantee my mouth will cooperate once I try to get it out.

"You should tell S-S-S...tell him." I take a sip of my drink and then smile at Nolan. "He's the brains behind the whole thing. I'm not s-sure how I got s-s-s...dragged into this."

"'Cause you're brilliant and know a lot more about distributing books than I do," Sterling butts in.

That's debatable. Just because I own a bookstore, that Sterling works in as my sole employee, doesn't mean I know jack shit about jack shit. My grandpa left me a pile of money and even more books. Opening a bookstore was the only thing I could think to do with them. I love my quirky little indie bookshop, but that doesn't mean I know a damn thing when it comes to mobile libraries or much of anything else.

"I know a l-lot about r-r-reading books, but

—" Before I can finish what I'm about to say, the air in the room feels like it shifts. Maybe I'm a tad dramatic, but I swear it's like a movie moment where everything stands still and the camera zooms in on the Adonis of a man who just stepped into the room.

Kiernan

I unfasten the button on my suit jacket and reach up to loosen the constricting tie around my neck while I sweep the busy kitchen to make sure everything is in order for Barrett's birthday party. Not that I don't trust his boy to handle it, and I have no doubt he enlisted Nolan's help to plan the perfect party, but what can I say? I can't rest easy until I feel like I have control of any given situation. A therapist would likely have a field day with me, given my issues with my father and the fact that I like men to call me Daddy—both in bed and out—but it works for me, and I'm not enlisting any professional opinions on the matter at this point.

Everything seems to be in order: cake, finger foods, alcohol… I would've hired waiters and a bartender, but given where Sterling came from not long ago, I doubt it crossed his mind to hire staff for the party.

Speaking of Barrett's sweet boy, I spot him near the alcohol station, apparently conversing with Nolan and my sweet little unicorn himself...*Emerson.*

I take a second to enjoy the sight of him before he notices I'm here. His face has a lovely tan, his features relatively relaxed as he takes a sip from his glass. His lips are so pink I have to wonder if he puts anything on them—lipstick, lip gloss—if not, would he consider it if I asked nicely? I groan quietly at the thought of the boy kneeling between my thighs, letting me paint his lips an even more eye-catching shade than they already are.

Then again, it would be an utter shame to hide his natural features. Maybe something clear and shiny instead...

"He's not on the menu," Alden says in a deadpan tone, sidling up beside me and following my gaze.

"Says who?" I ask.

That's when the boy notices me, his attention shifting from his friends and zeroing in on me, his cheeks turning bright pink in an instant. I can't deny that it's heady to see visual proof of the effect I have on him. The problem is that I can't tell if it's attraction or if he's intimidated by me for some reason.

"Says Barrett," my business partner and friend reminds me.

"Well, that would be a problem if I were Sterling. But last I checked, Barrett isn't the boss of me." I smirk and start across the room toward the beverages, suddenly absolutely parched.

Emerson's breath appears to quicken as I approach. He takes another sip of his drink, spilling some of it down his chin and then wiping it with the back of his hand with an utterly flustered expression on his face. Adorable.

Most everyone in attendance is wearing dress shirts, if not designer suits, but not him. He's wearing jeans and a purple unicorn T-shirt. I'm starting to wonder if he has a closet full of them or if he wears this particular shirt special just for me. I rather like the idea of the latter. My cock thickens at the idea of the boy dressing with me in mind, even if we've only exchanged a few words of conversation and I have no right to such fantasies.

"Emerson," I purr his name when I reach him, and the blush on his cheeks deepens.

Instead of saying anything in response, he takes another deep gulp from his drink, nearly polishing the entire thing off in one go. He casts a glance full of pleading in Sterling's direction, and my previously stirring cock deflates. Maybe he *is* afraid of me. I can't think of any reason for him to feel that way, but I have been told on more than one occasion that I have a rather intimidating presence before you get to know me.

Before I can decide on my next move, Sterling checks his phone and grins. "He's pulling up right now. Everybody has to hide."

"Hide?" Alden repeats, arching an unamused eyebrow.

"Of course. It ain't no surprise if he walks in here to find us all standin' around in the kitchen," he reasons, fixing a determined expression on his face that says he's not about to back down on this.

I guess we're all going to hide.

Everyone begins to disperse to the living room to duck behind furniture without any dignity or elegance. It's a bit of fun, if I'm honest, to see all of these well-to-do, well-dressed people crouching on the floor in the dark.

I find myself behind the armchair, shoulder to shoulder with Emerson. It wasn't planned, but I'm certainly not complaining about the turn of events. Given his reaction to my earlier approach, I do my best not to make him feel too crowded in the confined space. Still, I can't help but notice the comforting smell that seems to be wafting off of him. He smells like a quiet summer night, like peace and relaxation. There's something so sweet about it, that it's not cologne or anything artificial. A smile curves on my lips. ... he smells like books.

It makes me want to find out more about him. Who is Emerson aside from the adorable, unicorn-loving bookstore owner? As silly as I feel hiding behind a chair, possibly ruining my expensive pants, I would gladly stay cloistered back here the rest of the night just to get the chance to talk to him, to find out if I could coax a few words out of him.

He turns his head a fraction, like he's trying to look at me without being too obvious. In my mind, I run through a thousand things to say —clever things, funny things, dirty things—but before I have a chance to settle on any of them, the front door opens.

"I'm home, Pretty Boy," Barrett calls out, lights flickering on as his footsteps grow near. "Are you sitting in the dark?"

The living room light comes on, and we all pop out of our hiding places and shout, "Surprise!" The look on Barrett's face is priceless, and I have to admit that Sterling was right; it *was* a lot more fun to hide for the surprise.

Sterling runs over and jumps into Barrett's arms. He stumbles back a little but catches his boy with relative ease and kisses him senseless. A pang of longing zings through my chest, watching the two of them in a sweet lip-lock before they part and just *smile* at each other for a few seconds with these sweet, dopey grins that would be a little nauseating if I didn't want what they have so damn badly.

Barrett sets him down, and that's apparently a signal for the party to really start. Someone starts some music, and people begin to congregate around the food, booze, and birthday boy.

"Do you want another drink?" I offer Emerson, nodding toward the empty glass in his hand. He looks down at it as if he's surprised to realize he finished the entire thing already.

After a few seconds, he nods and offers me the glass. "Thank y-y-y…" His cheeks pink again, and he clamps his lips shut.

"You're welcome." I take the glass. "Martini?" I guess.

He wrinkles his nose and shakes his head quickly. "Vodka and S-S-SS-Sprite."

Emerson looks embarrassed again, and I'm not sure if it's because he thinks his stutter is something to be ashamed of, or he assumes I'm judging his choice of drink. He couldn't be more wrong about either.

When I reach the drink station, Barrett's there, mixing two drinks.

"Happy birthday, man," I say, using my free hand to pull him into a hug and pat him on the back.

"Thanks. I can't believe Sterling pulled this all together without me knowing about it." He smiles fondly and shakes his head. I've known Barrett most of my life, and I've never seen him as happy as he's been since he met his boy. As envious as I am, I'd be a complete and utter dick if I weren't also over the moon thrilled for my best friend.

"He's a good one," I agree, squeezing his shoulder one more time and then grabbing the vodka and Sprite for Emerson's drink.

"Since when is that your drink?" he asks, eyeing me curiously.

"It's not for me."

He sighs, and I bristle a little. Doesn't the man have his hands full with his own boy without worrying about who I'm interested in?

"He's really sweet and innocent as hell," he reminds me as if we haven't had this conversation a dozen times since he brought Em into the office six months ago to give a presentation on mobile libraries that we all agreed to invest in. "Not to mention, we're financial backers for this mobile library project, which makes things very murky from an ethical standpoint. You wouldn't want him to feel pressured into anything."

"Does Sterling feel pressured by our financial backing?" I counter.

"That's different. We were together before the firm invested in their idea," he reasons, and I snort. Clearly, I'm not going to argue him out of this idea that he needs to protect Em from my big, bad Daddying.

"I hear you," I finally say, just to end the lecture. "It's just a drink, not a collar or a ring, okay?" I pour myself a bourbon, and Barrett nods.

It's a moot point, anyway, considering there's still an even chance the boy is absolutely terrified of me. And even if he wasn't, I have no idea if he's interested in the lifestyle at all. This could all very well be a dead-end crush.

CHAPTER 2

Emerson

I stumble out of the Uber outside of my apartment building, stuttering a thank you to the driver and then fumbling in my pockets in search of my keys.

I didn't plan to drink that dang much, but every time I held my empty glass out to Kiernan, he offered to get me a refill instantly. There was something incredibly heady about the way he jumped to take care of me over and over with little more than a look. I'm sure he was only being polite, but it didn't stop my stomach from fluttering and my cock from getting excited about the whole thing. Unfortunately, that meant I drank *way* too much and had to get an Uber home. Not my finest moment.

Kiernan offered to drive me, but I clammed up and blushed so hard I'm surprised I didn't faint, and then I shook my head no without thinking. It's for the best anyway, god knows the ways I would've found to embarrass myself if I'd accepted a ride from him.

I keep one hand on the wall to prevent the hallway from spinning as I make my way up to the second floor.

I barely had the courage to say more than a few words to Kiernan all night, but for some reason, he still stayed close, always seeming to be watching me. Not in a creepy way...in a very hot, very *not* creepy way. So basically, I'm drunk and horny and now home all alone.

Story of my fucking life.

I clumsily kick off my shoes as soon as I'm inside my apartment, letting the door swing closed behind me. I drop my keys haphazardly and shuffle straight for my bedroom, absently palming my half-hard cock through my jeans. I spent half the night spinning impossible fantasies in my mind starring the giant ginger deity, and now I want to do something about them. Well, I want to do *two* things about them.

As soon as I'm in my bedroom, I strip out of my tight jeans, so I'm more comfortable, and then I climb into bed. It takes me a minute to arrange my pillows, so they're propped up against the headboard. Then I reach over to grab my laptop off my nightstand, my mind already conjuring the words my fingers are itching to type.

Long before I owned the bookstore, I started another career. A secret career I have to this day…

I open the doc I've been working in and quickly fall right back into the story of a shy, secretly filthy boy being seduced by a Daddy who looks remarkably like a Viking. People always say to write what you know, after all.

My fingers fly over the keys, setting the scene with the two main characters being thrown together at a party for a mutual friend. That's where the similarities to real life leave off and my own fantasies take over.

The boy in the story decided to be very naughty before the party and put in his favorite remote-controlled vibrating butt plug. The only problem is, he's lost the remote and is now desperately trying to find it before someone else does. *Oh, you sweet boy, you are in for a ride.* I imagine myself and Kiernan in place of the characters, and I grin wickedly as the Daddy stumbles on the remote and starts to work out what it is.

"No, no, no. It has to be here somewhere," Paul mutters frantically, doing his best to retrace his steps through the house. He's sure he had it when he arrived. He'd stood on the front porch and fingered the remote in his pocket, getting hard at the thought of no one knowing his dirty little secret. That's the last time he can remember having it though.

He clenches around the plug, feeling an odd sort of comfort from the fullness of it. It's seated against his prostate, the perfect size to vibrate right against his bundle of nerves if he presses the button. In fact, every step he takes has the toy rubbing against him, keeping him horny all night long.

Paul shuffles down the hallway to the bathroom, hoping the remote fell out of his pocket when he used it earlier. But the bathroom is bare. He sighs in frustration, leaning against the sink and closing his eyes. He doesn't even hear the creek of the door open until Leif's large form is filling the doorway.

Paul peeks one eye open and finds the tall, broad, mouth-watering man with something in his hand.

"Missing something, sweetheart?" he asks with a wicked smirk, pressing the button. The toy vibrates to life inside Paul, sending a jolt through his body.

"Ooh," he moans, clutching the sink tighter, his cock jerking and his whole body heating all at once.

"You know, you should really be more careful where you leave these types of things." Leif presses the button again, ramping up the vibration until Paul is panting and fighting back desperate moans, shamelessly canting his hips and biting into his bottom lip.

I groan at my own words on the screen, pulling one hand off the keyboard to shove it into my own underwear, sighing at the relief of wrapping my fingers around my aching cock. My nipples are hard, rubbing against the soft fabric of my T-shirt, my skin hot and my hole fluttering jealously at not being filled like the boy in the story.

As my eyelids drift closed, I let myself pretend for a second that Kiernan really was looking at me with lust tonight. That he would happily corner me in a bathroom and force me to orgasm over and over until my underwear is absolutely soaked with cum, and I'm begging him to take pity on my over-sensitive prostate and achingly empty balls.

My cock jerks in my fist, and I shove my laptop aside, spreading my legs and stroking myself faster. My breath speeds up, too, my body thrumming and my balls tightening from the impossible fantasy I've lost myself in.

I gasp and moan, thrusting into the tunnel of my hand as I picture Kiernan's eyes clouded with lust, a large bulge in the front of his own pants as he cranks up the vibrations again until I fall to my knees in front of him and come one last time, sobbing and breathless and utterly spent.

I cry out, my cock pulsing in my grip as cum spills over my knuckles and makes my underwear wet and sticky. I stroke myself until my cock starts to soften, and then I slip out of my underwear, using them to mop up the rest of my cum before tossing them aside.

I wish I could say I feel better after coming my brains out, but I feel strangely empty and more than a little lonely.

Not in the mood to write anymore, I reach over and close my laptop. Then I pull my body pillow to my chest and cuddle it tight, closing my eyes and pretending it's the Daddy I've spent years dreaming of. He never had a face before, just a strong, gentle, perfect man who would love me. He has a face now, but I doubt it will ever be anything more than a fantasy.

Kiernan

My footsteps echo eerily through my empty house as I walk down the hall, loosening the buttons on my shirt as I make my way toward my bedroom. When I bought this house ten years ago, I imagined extravagant kink parties with beautiful boys, adorable puppies, blushing subs, and every manner of adoring Dom filling the multitude of rooms and spilling out onto the pool deck out back. That dream has come to fruition more times than I can count, ghosts of parties past still imprinted in my memory.

In the last year, I've grown a bit tired of

the parties. In fact, in the last twelve months, I've held only one.

I reach my bedroom and sit down on the foot of my custom-made bed, twenty-five percent larger than a California King and just about the most comfortable thing in existence. I pull off one shoe, then the other, and then finish unbuttoning my shirt so I can shrug it off.

I might have bought the place with a dream of filling it with fun and friends, but the only thing I can think of now when I look around my empty rooms is how much I want a boy of my own to share my home and my life. I want what Barrett has with Sterling. I want it so badly that my chest literally aches with it when I let myself think about it too hard.

Once I've stripped down to my boxers, I pick up my phone and frown at the lack of notifications. Not that I was expecting any, not rationally anyway. But when Sterling put a drunk and sloppy Emerson into an Uber, I itched to demand the boy text me to let me know he got home safe. Of course, I *didn't* do that because it's not my place. Hell, he looked absolutely petrified when I offered to give him a ride myself, which is a big enough sign that I should back off and get over this crush.

With a sigh, I climb into bed. It's late, and it's been a long damn day, but my brain isn't quite ready to sleep yet. I prop one arm under my head and pull up my M4M app out of habit, navigating right to the kinky section and scrolling absently for boys in my area.

I've never had any trouble finding partners. Right now, there are dozens of boys active online, advertising that they're looking for a spanking or a quick and dirty fuck. I could message any of them, and no doubt have company in minutes flat. I'm good-looking and, apparently, red hair is *in* at the moment. And even if I wasn't a fox, my money is more than enough to draw boys in like bees to honey. But no amount of good looks or zeros in my bank account has gotten me the *right* boy yet.

I scroll for a few more minutes, not truly looking, just going through the motions of a decade-long habit before closing the app and tossing my phone aside.

I'm too restless to sleep and not in the mood to find a hookup or jerk off… Another drink might do the trick; I only had one at the party. But considering my father was an alcoholic, I try not to get into the habit of letting alcohol solve any of my problems.

With an irritated grunt, I throw back my covers and climb back out of bed. There's only one solution tonight. Well, two solutions, but calling Sterling and demanding to know where

Emerson lives so I can drive over there and make sure he got home safe isn't an option, at least not a rational one.

I get out of bed and strip my underwear off, tossing them into the pile with the rest of my discarded clothes. One of the things I loved the most about this house when I bought it was that the master bedroom has a door that leads to the pool out back.

It's a warm night, the smell of the pool and summer air filling my lungs as I step outside. My house is far enough outside the city that there's a beautiful array of stars overhead and plenty of privacy.

I clearly have a one-track mind tonight because even as I approach the pool, getting ready to dive into the lukewarm water, I imagine Emerson wet and naked, splashing in the pool and beckoning me to join him for a swim.

How have I developed such an obsession with a boy I hardly know? Am I truly shallow enough that his adorable T-shirts and sinful lips are enough to inspire such single-minded thoughts of him?

I dive into the water, the slight chill of it enough to clear some of my thoughts. I quickly lose track of how many laps I swim, back and forth, until my muscles are aching and the restlessness is starting to ease out of me. I'm also graced with enough clarity to see that the only true solution to this little obsession of mine is to get to know Emerson better. Either it will cure me of the fantasy I'm holding of him, or I'll get the chance to woo him. I would consider either outcome a win at this point.

With a plan in place and my energy spent, I get out of the pool and grab a towel to dry off. This time, when I fall into bed, sleep pulls me under. Of course, even then, I have dreams of the boy I'm not sure I'll ever have.

CHAPTER 3

Emerson

I shuffle through my morning routine, guzzling down coffee and helping customers with a tired smile on my face. I've been up way too late the past few nights in a row, writing and thinking about a certain ginger man I really shouldn't be thinking about.

I yawn and shoot the woman I'm ringing up an apologetic smile before bagging her books and handing her the receipt.

"T-thanks for coming to Unicorn B-b-b-books." She's barely out the door before another yawn stretches my jaw.

"Late night?" Sterling asks, waggling his eyebrows at me. When we first met, he was so shy; now he assumes every sleepless night is the fun kind. That Daddy of his has corrupted him, I swear. And by the smile on his face, I'm pretty sure he likes it.

"Yes, b-but not for any fun reason." Unless you count writing a five-thousand-word sex scene and then riding my dildo until I passed out at three in the morning to be fun. It wasn't *not* fun, but it definitely would've been more if I hadn't been all alone.

"Bummer." He returns to shelving the new stock of books we just got in.

The bell over the door jingles and I paste on a fresh smile and turn to greet the new customer.

"W-w-welcome to Uni—" The words dry up on my lips when my brain registers who just walked through the door. Kiernan is taking in the store with an appraising eye while all six and a half feet of solid muscle and wild red hair fills my doorway.

"Emerson," he purrs my name in a way that heats me up from head to toe, making me all the more flustered and unable to unstick my tongue from the roof of my mouth. "Nice place." He grins, giving the small store another quick once-over and then striding toward the counter.

Shit, shit, shit. My face is burning hot, my stomach twisting itself in knots as I try not to hyperventilate. For the life of me, I can't figure out why this man, in particular, makes me *so* nervous. I'm never *great* around hot men, but I can usually get out enough words and keep myself from having a full-on meltdown long enough to get them into bed.

Maybe it's because he's the first Daddy I've knowingly interacted with. I don't just want to get words out; I want them to be the right words.

"I was hoping you could help me. I've joined an online book club, and it's my turn to choose the book for us to read, and I'm blanking on everything other than kinky, gay erotica." He lowers his voice on the last few words, adding enough weight to them that they feel like they're reaching out and effortlessly stroking my cock to life.

I shift closer to the register, hoping the counter will hide the bulge forming in the front of my jeans.

"W-w-wwww…" The first word gets stuck, and my skin starts to prickle with anxiety, making it that much harder to try again. I lick my lips and swallow around my dry throat. "G-genre?"

I hate myself for having to resort to grunting a one-word question, but it's far less embarrassing than stumbling and stuttering my way through anything more complete.

"That's where I'm struggling. So far, the picks have been rather… Well, I'll just say it, *depressing*. I want something a little more fun but with enough meat that we can have a good discussion about it."

I know just the book for him. It came out

a few weeks ago, and I've already read it half a dozen times. I want to gush about it, to tell him why it's my new favorite book, about how the protagonist, who's desperately trying to find meaning in his life as a twenty-two-year-old gay man with no direction and no plans, ends up accidentally driving the getaway car for a bank robbery, stumbles onto a tour with a rock band, and then finds himself the unwitting leader of a cult, among other zany adventures that ultimately teach him about life and love and himself.

I don't say any of that because I don't trust myself to get any of it out. Instead, I nod and come around the counter, making a beeline for the shelf where I have copies of *Confessions of a F*ck-Up* and hand one to him. Kiernan flips the book open to read the description and then peruses the first couple of pages. I watch him shamelessly, my heart fluttering wildly at the amused grin that forms on his lips from the very first sentence.

"This seems perfect. Thank you." He shuts the book and leans against the shelf, looking me up and down brazenly before tucking the book under his arm and straightening up.

I'm still working on getting my tongue to cooperate as I head back to the register to check him out. I cast a quick glance around, wondering where Sterling disappeared to.

"I meant to ask you at Barrett's party the other night," Kiernan says, pulling out his wallet and handing me his credit card to run. "I'd love to take you for coffee sometime."

Coffee? He wants to take me for coffee? I will my mouth to form the word *yes* but end up stumbling over the "e" sound as it drags across my lips and gets stuck.

To Kiernan's credit, he stands patiently, not frowning or making irritated noises like some people have done in the past. He simply *stands* and waits. I lick my lips and try again, but I'm too nervous, my whole body feeling hot and cold all at once.

I huff in frustration and shake my head sharply. He seems to misinterpret that as my answer to his offer for a date. He frowns just a fraction before putting on a good-natured smile and straightening up. "If you ever change your mind…" He takes his credit card back and hands me a business card instead.

I take it with a shaky hand, hating my mouth and my brain for screwing me out of this date. He grabs the book, and I curl my fingers tight around the business card so I don't accidentally lose it. I watch as he leaves, and only then does my tongue manage to unknot itself.

"S-s-sssss-Sterling," I shout.

My now *ex*-best friend pops up from behind the bookshelves with a would-be innocent expression on his face. "Super busy back here. Did I miss somethin'?" He feigns innocence, and I shoot him a look to cut the shit while waving Kiernan's business card in his direction.

"What do I d-d-do?"

He comes around the shelves to join me at the front. Sterling hops up onto the counter and taps his chin like he's considering the situation. "Gonna go out on a limb here and say you should call."

"Ha," I bark out a laugh and shove the card into my back pocket. "F-f-f-fat ch-chance."

"Why not?"

I give him another look. As if he wasn't eavesdropping behind that shelf, listening to what an absolute idiot I made of myself. I can't string two words together in front of him. How am I supposed to go on a date with him?

"I'm too n-nervous."

"Hm," he hums, seeming to give it some genuine thought this time. "You know what you need?"

"What?"

"Practice flirting with Daddies." Sterling waggles his eyebrows at me, and I give another harsh laugh.

"I'm s-s-sure other Daddies will be easier to talk to than he is," I say, my tone dripping with sarcasm.

"Online they would be," he reasons.

I scrunch my eyebrows together and then realize he's probably referring to the time I mentioned the kink section of M4M to him. "M-m-maybe."

"You deserve a Daddy who's crazy about ya."

My chest aches at the thought. I want that; I really do. Maybe it *would* be easier to get some practice chatting online. I can gain a bit of confidence, and then I'll be able to get up enough courage to say a full sentence in front of Kiernan.

"I'll think about it," I agree, and Sterling smiles.

CHAPTER 4

Kiernan

I straighten the lapels on my suit and then snag a glass off a waiter's tray as he hurries by. The champagne bubbles fizz against my tongue as I take a sip, surveying the crowded room.

I can't for the life of me remember what we're even fundraising for tonight. Some kind of medical research, maybe? A new cancer drug? No, that was two weeks ago...

I shake my head and take another sip of my drink. It doesn't matter. Whatever this is for, we'll raise the money we need, then contribute some of our own to make sure the project is funded, and I'll do all the legal paperwork.

It was with a grudging acceptance that I attended Harvard Law School, mostly as a way to make it up to my parents after coming out and shattering their dreams of having the family name carried on. Kids. *Shudder*.

Months before graduation, filled with pitiable rich boy ennui, Barrett came to me and pitched the idea of partnering to start an investment firm—my legal expertise and his money. He was sure we could change the world, put some good back into it, and I was sold on the idea. I just wish he'd warned me how many tedious parties we would have to attend.

"There you are, Daddy." My date, Henry, approaches with a flirty smile on his lips as he slides an arm around me. I didn't tell him to call me Daddy. In fact, I wish he would stop, which isn't a feeling I'm familiar with. Maybe it's because it sounds so manufactured. As if he's saying it because he thinks that's what I expect, not because he wants all of the attention and care that I'd offer him if I *were* his Daddy.

"Here I am," I say flatly, handing him my half-empty champagne flute. He takes a sip and leans into me, which irritates me for some reason. On the surface, he's being perfectly sweet; I'm not sure why it's grating on my nerves so much.

"I'm so glad you brought me here tonight. I've met so many interesting people. I'd love to come to more of these." He runs his hand up my arm and bats his long eyelashes at me. "But I might need more nice clothes, Daddy."

Ah, there it is.

I hum in acknowledgment, and he starts fishing for a Rolex while I proceed to tune him out. My eyes wander over to Barrett on the dance floor with his boy, smiling like a fool and swaying to the music. A sour feeling fills my stomach as I grimace and look away from their blinding display of pure love and joy.

A few feet away, sitting at a table by himself and seeming to peruse the crowd the same way I am, is Alden. He didn't bring a date tonight. In fact, he hasn't brought a date to an event in well over a year. With Henry continuing to blatantly angle for expensive trinkets, I have to acknowledge the wisdom of Alden's approach. Then again, as I watch his eyes greedily track the movements of Barrett's assistant, Gannon, across the room, I have to assume that he has his own reasons for steering clear of the dating pool recently.

"Don't you think, Daddy?" Henry asks.

"Not really," I answer, not bothering to wonder what it was he asked. His face hardens into a glare, so I guess it was the wrong response. If only I had it in me to give a shit. "I think I've had enough for one night."

His face lights up again, and he puts a hand on my chest, puckering his lips in a look that I think is meant to be sexy but just makes him look like he has a duck face. "You want to take me back to your place, Daddy?"

"I'm going to take you home, Henry, and

then I'm going to go back to my place...alone."

He sticks his bottom lip out in a pout. "I'd love to take a dip in your pool. The only thing is, I don't have a swimsuit with me." I've gotta give it to him; he's really trying. There's no telling what he would do if I *did* buy him a Rolex or whatever car he was hinting about while I ignored him. That's just the thing though, I've had about all I can take of boys who only want me for what's in my wallet.

"No," I say firmly.

He crosses his arms defiantly. "Maybe I'd rather find someone else to take me home then."

I huff through my nose in irritation. "Suit yourself. Have a good night."

I would slip some cab money into his pocket just to be safe, but based on the way a few of our wealthy donors are eyeing him, I don't think he'll have any trouble finding what he's looking for tonight.

I find my car and driver parked around the back. Jordan gives me a rather pitying look when he sees that I've lost my date at some point in the night and opens the car door for me.

"Home?" he checks.

I consider the question for half a second. Is there somewhere else I could go to ease the aching loneliness in my chest? The answer used to be Ball and Chain, the kink club just outside of town, but the boys there aren't much different than Henry. They see me coming a mile away and flock to me with dollar signs in their eyes.

"Home," I say with a sigh. Jordan nods and doesn't say another word as he takes me back to my big, empty house.

As soon as I'm inside, I follow my familiar routine of heading for my bedroom and stripping down to my underwear.

Em turned me down, and every other boy in Las Vegas is just out for my money. Maybe I should wander into the first backwater bar I find and see if fate decides to bless me the way it did Barrett.

What I really need is the chance to meet boys before they know who I am. If I could get to know someone without my money clouding everything, maybe then I could have the kind of relationship Barrett found with Sterling.

I pick up my phone to clear all of my M4M notifications and the texts from Barrett and Alden asking where I disappeared to. Then an idea occurs to me. M4M...

I open the app and log out of my profile. I hover my thumb over the Create New Profile button, wondering if this idea has any merit before deciding there's only one way to find out.

Emerson

I pace back and forth in front of my open laptop. I've been trying to work up the courage to click Done on my new kink-specific profile for about half an hour now. I *would* text Sterling for a pep talk, but he's at some fancy party tonight.

Kiernan is probably there too, no doubt with a fabulous date on his arm. A date that could have been me if I didn't freeze up last week when he asked me to go out for coffee with him. My options were to either spend the night pouting and eating ice cream or take Sterling's advice and get some practice in with Daddies online until I'm comfortable enough to be brave in front of Kiernan. I ate an entire carton of ice cream, and now, here we are.

"You can do it," I whisper to myself before taking a deep breath and leaning over my laptop. "Just p-press the button."

I decided to make a new profile so I could limit the personal information I included. Everything I wrote is real, I just kept it a lot vaguer than my regular profile. I did the same with my profile pictures: none of my face, just some artsy body images.

I clench my eyes closed and stab the enter

button with my index finger, letting out a little "eep" that I *think* is relief but is possibly pure terror now that I officially have a profile up on the M4M: Kink.

I'm not sure what I was expecting to happen, but it's pretty anticlimactic. Some suggestions for men in my area start to pop up, but that's it. Once my heart starts to beat at a more normal speed, I climb onto my bed, folding my legs into a pretzel, and pull my laptop closer so I can browse.

There are more Daddies than I expected. Although, I guess it *is* a big city and some of them are likely tourists here for some weekend fun. There's a huge variety: strict Daddies, doting Daddies, old, young, chubby, skinny... My mind spins over all of the options I have to sift through.

I've known I was into the idea of having a Daddy since I was sixteen and stumbled onto some Daddy porn, but I haven't given thought to all the different kinds of Daddies there would be to choose from. How am I supposed to know what I like or what I want?

I scan profile after profile, learning things I'm stunned to realize I never thought of before. Like how some Daddies are only Daddies in bed and others want it twenty-four-seven. Which do I want? I think I might like spanking, but what about other kinds of punishments?

Not only do I feel like I'm in over my head with this, but I'm starting to wonder if I'm a really shitty writer for not realizing all of the nuances of this lifestyle. In my defense, my only *research* for my books is porn and my own fantasies.

I'm about to slam my laptop closed and call this a failed experiment when a message pops up.

LonelyDaddy: Hi.

LonelyDaddy: I love the unicorn tattoo you have in your profile pic.

BraveBoy: It's a Pegasus. Unicorns have horns, Pegasus have wings, and if it has both, it's an Alicorn.

LonelyDaddy: I stand corrected. I had no idea.

BraveBoy: Come for the kink, stay for the useless factoids about mythical creatures.

LonelyDaddy: Ha! That genuinely made me laugh, thank you.

I grin and click on his profile picture so I can see the rest of his info. His profile is similarly vague. It says he lives here, but his profession is left blank. He's been in the lifestyle twenty years, and he wants a full-time boy. Like me, he doesn't have any pictures of his face, but the body shots are more than enough to pique my interest. My favorite is a photo of his chest that looks broad and sturdy, covered in auburn chest hair.

It reminds me of Kiernan, and my stomach jolts, wondering if it could be him. I'm sure he has a profile on this site. Who doesn't? I navigate back to the full list of men in my area, scrolling quickly to see if I can spot anyone else who could be Kiernan. Sure enough, the second page has a profile that's unmistakably him. The main image is his smiling face, and his username is Ginger-Daddy.

Disappointment settles in my stomach, but before I can wallow in it, another message pops up from my new friend.

LonelyDaddy: Your profile is pretty blank. What are you into, BraveBoy?

BraveBoy: Can I be honest with you?

LonelyDaddy: Please.

BraveBoy: I'm not totally sure what I'm into. I want a Daddy, and I definitely have some fantasies, but I haven't tried any of them out.

BraveBoy: That's kind of why I created this profile, I guess. I've been too nervous to meet any Daddies, and this felt like a safe first step.

LonelyDaddy: Chatting can be a fun way to learn about your preferences and kinks. I'm selfless enough that I'd be happy to help you out with that;)

BraveBoy: Lol, very selfless, thank you.

BraveBoy: I have a question...

LonelyDaddy: Shoot

BraveBoy: How do I figure out if I want a Daddy all the time or just in the bedroom?

LonelyDaddy: Full-time Daddies tend to be very hands on. When I have a boy, I'm serious about wanting to be involved in every aspect of his life, giving him structure like chores around the house, making sure he's eating, sleeping, and taking care of himself, solving his problems when I can, basically taking care of all of his needs.

I picture what he's describing, putting Kiernan in the Daddy role, of course. I let myself fantasize about coming home at the end of the workday to my big, strong Daddy scooping me up and carrying me to the couch so he can take my shoes off for me and rub my feet. A relaxed feeling flows through me as I imagine what it would be like to have someone I could trust and rely on to take care of everything for me. I would be so grateful to him. I would do everything I could to be his good boy in return.

A shiver of happiness runs through me.

BraveBoy: That's what I want.

LonelyDaddy: It's a beautiful thing to find.

BraveBoy: I'll have to work up the courage to meet a Daddy first. My username is kind of meant to be aspirational.

LonelyDaddy: Tell you what, I'm happy to be like training wheels for you. We can chat, and you can ask me any questions you want.

BraveBoy: You want a silly, nervous boy bothering you with stupid questions all the time? What's in it for you?

Nude pictures wouldn't be too big of a price to pay for the kind of help he's offering, but I'd like to know up front what he expects from me.

LonelyDaddy: First Daddy lesson: a true Daddy will do just about anything for the simple satisfaction of knowing he's taking care of a boy in need.

My throat tightens and my pulse thrums in my veins. That's the kind of Daddy I want.

LonelyDaddy: Now, do you have any more immediate questions, or can I ask some follow-ups about the Pegasus/unicorn distinction? Since you're clearly an expert and all…

I giggle at the message and type back a reply.

BraveBoy: Buckle up because I'm about to teach you everything you never wanted to know about mythical horses.

LonelyDaddy: Bring it on.

CHAPTER 5

Emerson

I yawn and try to focus on whatever it is that Sterling is going over. Something about refurbishing some old school buses we managed to get cheap. Fuck, I'm tired. I rub my eyes discreetly and fight back another yawn.

"Em?" Sterling says, and I look up from the paper I've been trying to concentrate on, all the numbers and dates swimming in front of my exhausted eyes.

"S-s-s-sorry, what?"

"I was just checking that you like the plan."

"Oh, yeah, it sounds g-great." I nod enthusiastically, glancing over at Gannon and Nolan, who occupy the loveseat opposite my chair. They don't look convinced that I was paying the least bit of attention and neither does Sterling.

"Is everything okay? If you hate this plan, we can talk about different options. That's the whole point of these meetings: to brainstorm together. I sure as heck don't have the first clue what I'm doin' here on my own." Sterling gives one of those cute, self-deprecating smirks.

"S-ss-sorry, I didn't get much sleep l-last night." I look at the paper again, skimming the information and then giving a reassuring nod. "This really does l-look great."

Sterling looks relieved and then glances over at Gannon. "You have a lot more experience with all this than I do. Does my timeline look good? Am I missin' anything?"

As Barrett's assistant, he's the only one of us with any real experience with launching non-profits. Apparently, a big part of his job is to oversee the early phases of many of the projects the company invests in.

"It looks good. But you might want to start talking to the various counties sooner rather than later. Bureaucratic paperwork can take ages," he advises, and Sterling makes a note on his own sheet of paper.

I have to wonder what help I am in any of this. Sterling seems to have a handle on the planning, Gannon is obviously useful, and Nolan is already hard at work planning some launch events and different things to bring community awareness to the mobile libraries once they're all ready to go.

"Our next biggest problem is figurin' out

how to get some books donated. It ain't gonna be a very impressive library without books."

I brighten up. Now *this* I can handle. "I can be in charge of that. I'll put up a donation b-b-bin at the shop, and I'll talk to other b-bookstores about doing the same. And I can set up social m-mm-media pages to support the cause as well."

"Great." Sterling makes another note and then closes the big binder he's keeping all of his paperwork in. "I think we're all set for tonight then. Anybody want snacks or anything?"

He stands up, and we all follow suit. Gannon struggles for a second, seeming to have a little trouble getting leverage on his prosthetic leg, thanks to how deep the sofa is. Nolan offers him a hand, and he scowls.

Nolan rolls his eyes. "Quit it with the macho pride shit and let me help you up."

Gannon grumbles for another few seconds, making another attempt to get up on his own before giving up and taking the offered hand. Nolan doesn't seem to give it another thought once Gannon is on his feet, flouncing after Sterling toward the kitchen. But I catch a tense look on Gannon's face, his square jaw clenched as he follows at a much slower pace. I notice a wince every few steps, and I wrestle with whether to mention it or not.

"Are you okay?" I finally check. If he wants me to fuck off, he can say that, but at least I'll have asked.

He breathes out through his nose, his nostrils flaring. "Fine, just sore."

I nod in understanding, dropping the subject as soon as we reach the kitchen where Sterling is already raiding the refrigerator and Nolan is pouring drinks.

Gannon leans against the counter, quietly watching Nolan, and I hover in the doorway, trying to figure out where I fit here. Do I belong at all, or am I just along for the ride because Sterling happened to wander into my bookstore his first day exploring Las Vegas?

Sterling looks up from assembling a fancy meat and cheese tray and waves me into the kitchen.

"So, you gonna tell us why you were up so late last night, or do we not wanna know?" he asks with a knowing grin.

My face heats while he and Nolan wait patiently for my answer. Gannon seems disinterested. I've gotten comfortable enough with the three of them that my stuttering usually isn't too bad when it's just us, but with all the attention aimed in my direction, I can already feel my tongue getting awkward and heavy before I've said a word.

"Chatting," I answer vaguely, coming the rest of the way into the kitchen to snag a piece of cheese off the tray.

"With?" Nolan asks, his pretty blue eyes dancing with curiosity as he leans forward and grabs some cheese as well.

"A D-D-D-Daddy on an app."

Sterling makes an excited noise, and Nolan tilts his head. Gannon continues to offer no comment. If it wasn't for the way he's watching Nolan slowly chew each bite of cheese, I'd wonder why he decided to stay for the post-meeting gossip session.

"Oh, lordy, you did it. Who is he? Is he hot? Do you like him? Is he nice?" Sterling shoots half a dozen questions at me rapid fire.

"He was nice." He was more than nice. We ended up messaging back and forth until nearly four in the morning. It was pretty innocuous, mostly sharing our interests, talking about movies and books, and a little bit of innocent flirting. I wonder if he'll message me again. If he really meant it when he said he would be happy to answer my questions and help me learn more about the Daddy kink lifestyle.

As if summoned by my thoughts, my phone vibrates in my pocket. My heart jolts and a smile jumps to my lips. I shove my hand into my pocket and pull it out. Sure enough, it's a message notification from M4M: Kink .

LonelyDaddy: Hey, BraveBoy. I have to tell you that I've been kicking myself all day for keeping you up so late last night. I hope you weren't too tired all day.

"That's him, ain't it?" Sterling guesses.

I shrug and type back a reply.

BraveBoy: I'm tired, but no regrets.

"Is he sexting you?" Nolan asks, waggling his eyebrows.

I bark out an embarrassed laugh, my face getting hot again, the feeling spreading down my neck and over my chest. "N-n-nnn-no."

"Really?" He doesn't seem convinced. "You're on a kink site chatting with him about oatmeal cookie recipes or something?"

"Daddy kink ain't just about sex," Sterling

says.

"H-he was apologizing for k-k-keeping me up too late and asking if I got enough s-sleep," I explain, resisting the urge to check the next message that just vibrated through my phone.

Nolan looks surprised and intrigued. "Wow. I guess I thought it was all sexy spankings and dirty talk."

"That's only part of it," Sterling tells him. "It's more about being taken care of."

"Huh," Nolan says.

Gannon reminds us of his presence with a skeptical sound in the back of his throat that he tries to cover by coughing. It seems like there's probably a story there.

"You gonna meet him?" Sterling asks.

"No, I'm doing w-what you s-ss-said. This is p-practice."

I give in to the urge to read the missed message.

LonelyDaddy: I'd love to chat later if you're free. Not too late tonight though, you need your rest.

BraveBoy: I'll be home in an hour.

LonelyDaddy: Talk soon then, sweet boy.

I smile at the affectionate pet name. I'm sure he doesn't mean anything by it, but it makes me feel special, just the way I always hoped a Daddy would make me feel. I can only imagine how much better it would feel to hear the words aloud, maybe whispered in a deep voice near my ear while my Daddy palms my cock through my pants.

A shiver runs through me, and I force the thought out of my mind for now. In an hour, I'll be at home chatting with LD. For now, I'm eating cheese with my friends and *not* getting a boner.

"So, Nolan, tell us about *your* love life," Sterling prompts, and we all turn our attention to the sparkly twink.

Kiernan

"Something interesting happening over there on your phone?" Alden asks in a bored drawl as he takes a sip from his expensive glass of scotch.

When it's clear BraveBoy isn't going to respond right now, I set my phone down and smirk across the table at my friend. "Nothing you need to concern yourself with."

"Hm, that means it *is* interesting." He curls his lips into what I'm sure is meant to be a smile but ends up looking more like a snarl.

"Do you have a new boy?" Barrett guesses, comfortably leaned back in his chair, taking a sip from his own drink.

"Yes and no," I answer vaguely, swirling my glass so the ice cubes clink against the sides. "He's a boy, and he's certainly new, but he's not *mine*."

"Oh?" Barrett prompts.

"I met him on M4M. He's new, like realized he's into Daddy kink by watching porn but hasn't dipped his toe into the waters yet kind of new."

Alden winces, and Barrett makes a noise in the back of his throat that pretty much sums up how I felt when BB told me that information. I'm as big a fan of porn as the next guy, but it's not often the best example of real-life relationships or kinks. In fact, I'd venture to say that boys who decide they want a Daddy based on some "call me Daddy while I ride you," rough-fucking, choke-on-my-cock porn clips are ripe for falling into relationships with men who have no business calling themselves Daddies at all.

"So, you're doing your good deed for the

month and educating the poor kid," Alden extrapolates.

"He's not a kid, but yes." I bounce my leg under the table, swigging back the rest of my drink and checking the time.

I'm sure Alden will be all too pleased to rib me about cutting our regular night out together short so I can rush home to chat with a boy who isn't even mine. Luckily, Barrett comes to my rescue, answering his own phone with a soft, dopey smile on his face that leaves no question about who's on the other end.

He talks softly for a minute or two before hanging up and tossing back the rest of his drink as well. "It's been a pleasure, gentlemen, but I have to be going."

"Horny, naked boy in your bed?" I guess.

Barrett gives a wolfish grin but refuses to confirm or deny, instead clapping us each on the back and taking off without a backward glance.

"I guess I should get going too." I stand up and button my suit jacket, running my hands down the front of the expensive, silky material to smooth it out.

Alden sighs and signals to the waitress for a refill. "Much easier to go home to an empty bed after the proper number of drinks," he explains when he notices my raised eyebrows.

Fuck do I understand that feeling, but I'm not sure I'm crazy about the idea of him using alcohol to deal with it. "There are lots of sweet, pretty boys who I'm sure would love to fill your bed."

He snorts. "You know sweet and pretty aren't my type."

I twist my lips in a condescending smile. "Fine, then I'm sure there are rugged, difficult boys interested in the position as well."

"Mm," he hums in what sounds like vague agreement, assessing me with his eyes. "This is my third drink, and it's not every night. I'm in a particular mood tonight, that's all." I appreciate the reassurance, but it doesn't make me worry that much less about him.

"You know I'm here if you need to talk, right?" I check, and he nods. "You're not the only one getting sick and tired of having a big, empty bed."

"I suspected I wasn't."

There isn't much else to say on the subject, so I simply nod. Alden lifts his glass in return, leaning back and crossing his ankle over his knee while he turns his attention to the quiet, upscale bar around us, a clear signal for me to leave him be.

My routine when I enter my house a

short time later is the same as always, except, this time, I find myself smiling, excited for the chance to chat with BB again. Last night, we barely touched on the subject of Daddy kink after our initial discussion. Instead we got to know each other a bit. He was absolutely sweet and delightful, and I kept him up entirely too late. Tonight, I'll make sure he gets to sleep at a proper time. I just want to hear about his day first. And if *that* doesn't prove just how damn lonely I've become, I don't know what will.

I strip down to my underwear and climb into bed. The silky fibers of my expensive bamboo sheets caress my skin, wrapping around me like an eager lover. If only.

I grab my phone and open the app, happy to see the little green dot by BraveBoy's profile indicating that he's online. There's one thing that's been niggling at the back of my mind all day…the tattoo in his profile picture.

I'm *sure* Emerson isn't the only gay man in Las Vegas with a penchant for mythical horses, but what if? I don't know enough about him to compare much else to what BB told me about himself. He likes books, but again, not exactly a smoking gun. He didn't share any pictures of his face or offer his real name, so if it *is* Emerson, he doesn't want anyone to know, and maybe that's all I need to know right now. The odds are slim, and it's likely nothing more than wishful thinking on my part.

BraveBoy: I'm home...

I smile as soon as the message pops up.

LonelyDaddy: Good. Are you nice and cozy in bed?

My message shows as read, and a few seconds later, an image pops up in the chat. It's a dimly lit room, the bare torso of a boy clearly reclining among a bed of sheets and pillows. The picture is hardly suggestive, but my cock perks up anyway, making me feel like a bit of a perv. He hasn't made the conversation sexual at all, and I offered to help him, which means I'm going to respect that.

Of course, that doesn't mean I can't send a picture in return. I follow his example, angling the camera on my phone so it only frames my bare, hairy chest, contrasted by the royal blue of my sheets.

BraveBoy: Wow. You look like you'd be nice to

cuddle.

LonelyDaddy: I am an expert cuddler. I know all the positions;).

BraveBoy: There are cuddle positions?! Please, enlighten me.

LonelyDaddy: Of course there are positions. You have your traditional spoon position, that one's a classic. But we mustn't forget lap pillow, chest pillow, leg braid, armpit tuck…

BraveBoy: Are those the official names? Is there a Cuddle-Sutra I don't know about?

LonelyDaddy: Not officially that I'm aware of, but if you encounter a Cuddle Master such as myself, I'm sure he'll be happy to show you his moves.

BraveBoy: See, I'm learning so much from you already.

LonelyDaddy: Glad to be of service.

BraveBoy: Speaking of sex…

LonelyDaddy: Were we speaking of sex?

BraveBoy: No, but I couldn't think of a better segue. Can I ask you a question?

LonelyDaddy: That's what I'm here for…

BraveBoy: Okay, so I'm not a virgin or anything, but I'm afraid that once I DO work up the courage to find a Daddy of my own that I won't know how to please him…you know, in bed. What do Daddies like?

LonelyDaddy: There's no blanket answer to that. Everyone is different. But what most Daddies REALLY like is to please their partner and the beautiful trust that submission shows.

BraveBoy: I can submit.

Even through the black and white font on the screen, I swear I can *feel* his eagerness. Like if he were in front of me, he would be absolutely vibrating to show me just how well he can follow directions, what a good boy he can be. My cock twitches again, tenting the front of my briefs.

LonelyDaddy: I'm sure you can, and I'm sure you'll make the right Daddy very happy when you're ready.

BraveBoy: What if I'm never ready? What if I'm too shy for the rest of my life?

LonelyDaddy: It's okay to be shy, especially when you don't know someone well. Yesterday, you probably felt nervous to chat with me when I first messaged, and now you're asking me sex questions.

BraveBoy: That's true, but it doesn't work as well in real life.

LonelyDaddy: Why not?

BraveBoy: It just doesn't...

LonelyDaddy: With the right Daddy, it will work.

My message shows as read, but he doesn't respond right away. Did I say something wrong? Eventually, the little dots pop back up to show he's typing a response.

BraveBoy: You're right. When it's right, it will work out. Thank you.

LonelyDaddy: No problem, beautiful boy.

BraveBoy: You don't know I'm beautiful. You haven't even seen me.

LonelyDaddy: I don't need to. You're beautiful on the inside, and that's what counts.

LonelyDaddy: It's getting late. I want you to get some sleep.

I half expect him to protest. After all, what right do *I* have to tell him what to do? As I told Alden and Barrett earlier, he's *a* boy, but he's not *my* boy.

BraveBoy: Yes, Daddy.

His response knocks the air from my lungs. I don't know what his voice sounds like, but I would kill to hear the words on his lips.

BraveBoy: I hope that was okay to say. After I sent it, I realized that it might be against protocol to call you Daddy when you aren't… you know…MY Daddy. It was just that telling me to go to bed was really Daddy-ish, and it felt right in the moment. I'm sorry.

LonelyDaddy: You can call me anything you like. Get some sleep and dream sweet things.

BraveBoy: Okay. I hope you sleep well too. Can we talk tomorrow?

LonelyDaddy: Count on it.

I log out of the app and set my phone down, the lonely ache in my chest somehow both better *and* worse after that chat.

Could BB become *my* boy? Is it possible we're building the foundation of something that could turn into more? I don't want to hang my hopes on anything just yet, but I *do* need to determine if BraveBoy could be Emerson before I get any more attached to either of them and things get complicated.

CHAPTER 6

Emerson

I flit around the bookstore with a song on my lips and a spring in my step, straightening the shelves and rearranging books that have been moved out of place by browsing customers. I did what LonelyDaddy said and went straight to sleep after we ended our chat. I wanted to get some writing in, and any other night, I would've pushed myself to stay up another few hours, ignoring my exhaustion just to write another chapter or two.

I'm glad I listened to him. Now I'm well-rested, and I can catch up on writing those chapters after I close the shop later. Daddies really are smart.

Longing fills my chest as I imagine how amazing it would be to have a full-time Daddy who was really all mine. He could make sure I got enough sleep. He could tuck me in and kiss me goodnight and then be there in the morning when I wake up. I sigh at the fantasy, still singing quietly to myself as I work.

I know he's only supposed to be practice, but I find myself thinking about LonelyDaddy. Who is he really? What's his name, and what does he do? What are his hobbies, and why doesn't he already have a boy of his own? But mostly about what it would feel like to crawl up next to him, lay my head on his big, furry chest, and let the sound of his heartbeat lull me to sleep.

Ugh, I feel like a flake. Two seconds ago, I was crushing hard on Kiernan, and now I can't stop daydreaming about a man I haven't even met. Maybe the crush on Kiernan was never real, he was just the first Daddy who paid any attention to me, and I latched onto it. After all, I don't exactly know the man. I already know more about someone I've chatted with online for two days than I know about him.

"Taylor Swift?" The sound of a familiar, deep voice filled with amusement startles a gasp from me, stopping me right in the middle of the chorus of "Invisible Strings."

"T-T-T-T-Taylor is Queen," I stutter out, raising a challenging eyebrow at Kiernan, who's peering at me over the Mystery section with a teasing smirk on his lips, daring him to argue with me.

"She's pretty good." He surprises me by agreeing. "I couldn't have a workout playlist without 'Shake it Off' on it."

A startled laugh bubbles from my lips. Did this giant, ginger beast of a man just say he works out to Taylor Swift? I bob my head eagerly in agreement, butterflies dancing in my stomach. Okay, so maybe I was trying to write off my crush on Kiernan a little too soon.

"C-c-can I help you w-w-w-w-with anything?" Even as I struggle to get the question out, I'm pretty sure it's the most words I've ever spoken to him in a row. That's progress, right? Maybe talking to LonelyDaddy really is giving me the confidence I've been needing. Baby steps, anyway.

I shelve the book I've been holding onto and head toward the front of the store.

"I was in the neighborhood," he answers vaguely, following a few steps behind me.

I scrunch my eyebrows, unable to hide my confusion. He was in the neighborhood and just decided to stop by? Why? I'm not exactly a rousing conversationalist when he's around. I can awkwardly shove more of my favorite books at him if he wants.

I'm not sure what I'm supposed to say in return, and the uncertainty makes my chest feel tight and my tongue feel heavy. I fidget with the hem of my shirt and then start compulsively nudging various items on the counter into only slightly different locations.

LonelyDaddy said it would be easier with the right person. Did he mean that I'd miraculously feel less uncomfortable and fidgety with the right man, or that the Daddy who's meant for me would know how to handle it and *make* it easier for me?

Points in Kiernan's favor, he simply stands there quietly, not pressing me to say anything or seeming particularly irritated with my nervous fidgeting.

"Can I ask you something?" He leans over the counter enough to bring him closer to me, but not enough to feel like he's encroaching on my personal space.

I nod, my pulse quickening. I hope whatever he asks doesn't require a long answer. Maybe he'll ask for a date again, and I'll be able to get the words out the right way this time.

"Do you have any tattoos?" His question startles me. Of all the things to ask, how did he come up with *that*? "I've been thinking of getting one," he goes on as if he can read my mind, or maybe he's just aware of how strange the question is.

So he wants a recommendation for a local artist? He wants to know if it hurts? What?

Whatever it is, revealing the slightly embarrassing fact that I have a Pegasus tramp stamp isn't going to help much. I didn't get it done locally, and I was drunk, so I have no idea if it hurt.

I give a quick shake of my head. "N-nnn-no."

His face falls, looking *way* more disappointed than I would've expected at my answer. Is the tattoo thing one of his kinks? Shit, maybe I should tell him the truth...

Before I get the chance, he puts on a fresh smile and stands up straight. "I should be going. I just wanted to stop by and say thank you for the book recommendation last time. It was excellent; I couldn't put it down."

A smile spreads over my lips. Is there anything more exciting than someone enjoying your favorite book? I can't think of a single thing. I hold up a finger to tell him to wait for a second, and then I hustle around the counter and over to the fiction section. It only takes me a second to find the book I'm looking for. It's a bizarre, dark-humor story with a very similar vibe to the one I gave him last time.

I take it over and hold it out to him. "Y-yy-you'll like this."

He doesn't bother to flip it open this time, just tucks it under his arm and pulls out his wallet.

"Between you and me, before I joined this book club, a majority of what I read was...well, basically porn," he confesses in a low whisper, a wicked smirk forming on his mouth. My eyes are drawn to the curve of his lips, and I can't help but wonder what his untamed beard would feel like against my skin. I squirm a little, imagining the chafe of beard burn on the insides of my thighs or between my ass cheeks.

If it was LonelyDaddy I was messaging with, and he said the same thing, I might share a confession of my own that I *write* gloriously filthy stories under a secret pen name. But I can't tell Kiernan that. Not only because I know there's no way I'd be able to get it out around my clumsy lips and tongue, but because it's too big of a secret, and I'm not sure what he would think. So instead I just blush and smile back, miming zipping my lips so he knows his secret is safe with me.

"Have a good day, Emerson." The way he says my name, caressing it with his mouth before he lets it fall from his lips, should be a crime, I swear.

He's already out the door before I manage to mutter, "You too."

I sag against the counter and bury my face in my hands. Another rousingly successful encounter.

Kiernan

I didn't realize until Emerson told me he didn't have any tattoos that deep down, I really thought he was BraveBoy. *Hoped* is more like. He's not, and I'm not sure how to feel about that or how I should move forward with the temptingly sweet boy who's just begging to be treated right by the Daddy of his dreams.

I lean back in my desk chair, absently stroking my thumb against the glossy cover of the hardcover book Emerson sent me off with today. My options are to either keep things platonic with BB and continue to hold out hope that Emerson's "no" about the date was out of nervousness rather than disinterest or to leave that crush in the past and see how things unfold with my mystery boy.

There are a million reasons the latter is the better option, the most important being that even if I got a "yes" from Emerson, I'm still not sure if he's into the lifestyle. BB could be everything I've been waiting for, and there's a strong connection there.

A rumble of irritation at my indecision vibrates through my chest.

"Sounds like someone's in a good mood today," Alden says. I look up to find him leaning against the doorway to my office.

"I'm in a fine mood." I push my book aside and swivel in my chair, waving him in. "What's up?"

"Just stretching my legs," he says, striding into my office. Instead of sitting, he walks over to the window, his hands in his pockets as he looks out. Why he wanted to look out my window rather than his own, god knows, but since he's here...

"Can I get your advice on something?"

"Yes, you should trim your beard. You look like a dock worker."

"Fuck off," I reply with a smirk. "I'm torn between two possible paths."

"You mean two possible boys?" he guesses.

"Mm," I grunt in agreement.

"Are both an option?" Alden asks, ticking one eyebrow up and nearly smirking.

"For one night of fun? Maybe if I played my cards right and wished on the right star. But I'm not looking to see how many boys I can fit into my bed all at once, I'm...I'm tired of being alone. I want someone permanent."

"Permanence and *one* are not mutually exclusive concepts, but we can leave that aside for now," he says. "I'm assuming your choices are between Emerson and this boy you met on the app?"

"Mm," I hum again, testing the bounce of my chair back by rocking a little as I jostle my knee.

"And you're going to choose this forever partner based on whoever *I* tell you to pursue?" he asks, his voice dripping with skepticism. When he puts it that way, it does sound ludicrous. "Your heart knows the right answer. And if it doesn't, then give it time and you'll figure it out."

"My heart knows the answer?" I repeat. "When did you start writing for Hallmark?"

"Fuck off," he replies without venom. "That's my advice, take it or leave it."

"Thanks."

He remains silent by my window for another minute or two, and I start to wonder if I should ask him if there's something on *his* mind. I've known the man for nearly two decades, and he's never been one to shy away from saying whatever he's thinking. He walks out as unexpectedly as he entered, and I make a mental note to ask Barrett if he knows what's going on with our friend.

In the meantime, I pull out my phone and send a message to BraveBoy.

LonelyDaddy: How's your day going, beautiful? Did you sleep well?

BraveBoy: I slept really well, and I'm having a good day.

BraveBoy: I think I slept TOO well though. I have too much energy.

LonelyDaddy: A good workout always helps me with that.

BraveBoy: You have no idea how badly I could use a good workout.

Even through text, the words are clearly *dripping* with innuendo. I grin at the words, compelled to test the waters of flirtation and see if he might be interested in more than simple friendship.

LonelyDaddy: Is that so, naughty boy?

I send the message and hold my breath, waiting to see if he takes the bait or steers things back to platonic joking. If he does, I'll take that as my signal to keep things as they are. But I think Alden was right. My heart knows what it wants, and fuck does it want BraveBoy to flirt back, to give me a sign he's open to exploring what might be between us.

BraveBoy: Yes. Solo workouts really aren't the same. They're never as satisfying.

LonelyDaddy: They can be if done properly...

BraveBoy: Hmm, maybe I need a personal trainer then;)

A litany of ideas fills my mind, ways I could play with him from afar until he's ready to take the next step and meet in person.

We chat awhile longer, exchanging innuendos and playful words until I let him go so I can get some work done, with a promise that we'll chat again tonight. A satisfied purr rumbles through my chest, knowing he'll be all mine again for the third night in a row. He said he got plenty of sleep last night, so I won't feel too bad about keeping him up late again.

I find myself smiling through the rest of the afternoon, counting the hours until my next chat with BraveBoy.

CHAPTER 7

Emerson

I'm dragging ass again today.

It's been two weeks since I started chatting with LonelyDaddy on the M4M app, and it's become a nightly routine I spend all day looking forward to. As diligent as he is about getting off the chat with me early enough for me to get a good night's sleep, the more I've chatted with him, the more inspired I've been to write each night. In the past two weeks, I've written half a dozen short stories. My fingers are actually starting to ache from how much I've been writing.

Kiernan hasn't stopped into the bookstore since the day he caught me singing and asked me about tattoos, which is weirdly both a relief and a major bummer.

The bell over the door jingles, and I look up to greet the newest customer with a friendly smile and wave and then return to dusting the nearest bookshelf. My phone vibrates in my pocket, and I dive to check it, a huge smile breaking out over my face when I see a new message from LonelyDaddy.

> **LonelyDaddy:** Hey there, sweet boy. How are you doing today?
>
> **BraveBoy:** Kind of boring, but otherwise, I can't complain.
>
> **LonelyDaddy:** There are worse things in life than boredom.
>
> **LonelyDaddy:** I wanted to run an idea by you…
>
> **BraveBoy:** Okay.

A zip of nervous energy rushes through me, wondering what he might be about to ask. Before I can find out, one of the browsing customers makes their way to the register. I put down my dust rag and hurry to check them out.

While I'm ringing them up, my phone vibrates several times in my pocket, making my pulse skyrocket, my fingers itching to get a hold of my phone and find out what it is LonelyDaddy wants to "run by me."

"C-come again," I say.

Of course, because I'm dying to know what

LD wants, all three of the other customers currently in the store all line up to check out at once. I do my best to keep a smile on my face, making brief small talk with one man who wants to tell me all about his favorite new book series. Normally, I'm *all* about book chat, but not when my phone is burning a hole in my pocket.

I whip out my phone the second the final customer steps away from the register.

LonelyDaddy: Let me buy you dinner tonight.

My hand starts to tremble, and I tighten my grip on my phone to keep from dropping it. When I didn't answer right away, he sent several follow-up texts.

LonelyDaddy: If you aren't ready to meet, I understand. I don't want to rush you.

LonelyDaddy: I have an alternative proposal if that's the case… I'll have a meal sent over to you, and we can have a virtual date, either over video or chat like we always do.

I grin at the messages, my anxiety melting away. Things have gotten flirty and a little romantic on our chats, but he's never pushed it, always letting me set the pace. And until now, I wasn't sure if we were just flirting as friends or if he could actually be interested in me.

BraveBoy: So...just to clarify, this would be like a date?

I nibble on my bottom lip while I wait for his reply. I know I'm not ready to meet him, and a video chat is out because he'd still have to suffer through my unbearable stuttering. My tongue is getting tired just imagining it. But the idea of sharing a meal, even if all we do is text during it, seems...sweet. Romantic.

LonelyDaddy: It would be exactly like a date.

A giddy feeling fills my chest, and I bounce happily on my toes for a second, doing a little dance. I'm glad Sterling isn't here to see me act this goofy over a man whose name I don't even know. I've wanted to ask him his name a hundred times over the past couple of weeks, but if I ask, then I'll have to tell him mine, and I'm just not ready.

That thought deflates some of my enthusiasm, and I finally get myself together enough to type a reply.

BraveBoy: I really want to say yes to a virtual date.

LonelyDaddy: What's stopping you?

BraveBoy: If I'm not ready to tell you my name or send you pictures of my face, am I ready for a date? Even if it is only virtual?

LonelyDaddy: I see your conundrum... What if I tell you I'm not ready to change what we have yet either? Let's take meeting off the table for now. We're just talking about taking the getting to know each other that we've been doing a little deeper.

BraveBoy: Okay...I like that. But I still feel weird agreeing to a date when I still refer to you as "LonelyDaddy" in my head...

LonelyDaddy: What if I tell you a name, but it won't be mine. And you can do the same.

BraveBoy: Like aliases?

I giggle at the suggestion, all of my insides warming at how sweet he's being.

LonelyDaddy: Like aliases.

BraveBoy: Okay, I'll be Tom.

LonelyDaddy: Nice to meet you, Tom. I'm Dick.

I burst out laughing, covering my mouth to muffle the sound and giving the man who just walked in an apologetic look.

BraveBoy: You can't be Dick.

LonelyDaddy: But my middle name is Richard...

BraveBoy: Pick a different name, Daddy.

LonelyDaddy: Mm, I'm fine if we just go with Daddy for now.

Another little thrill rushes through me.

BraveBoy: That works...Daddy.

LonelyDaddy: You're killing me, sweetheart. Do I get to hear your voice tonight?

BraveBoy: Not tonight. I hope that's okay. But I will give you my phone number. If we're going to have a proper date, you should have a way to contact me that isn't a hookup app.

LonelyDaddy: And your address so I can have food sent?

I chew on my lip again, considering the request. On the face of it, giving my address to a man I haven't met in person doesn't seem like the best idea. But LonelyDaddy...*Daddy* hasn't given me any reason not to trust him yet. He's been kind and respectful of my boundaries. He's been a perfect gentleman in every way.

I may not be brave enough to meet him just yet, but I think I have enough courage for this small leap of faith.

I send a message back with both my phone number and my address.

LonelyDaddy: I look forward to our date tonight. Expect food and a text at 7 pm.

BraveBoy: I can't wait.

Kiernan

Even if we won't be meeting in person tonight or even via video chat, I still take the time to dress for a date. It seems the right thing to do. I arranged delivery to both our addresses from my favorite little Italian bistro and paid a handsome tip to ensure the food arrives on time and still warm.

I arranged for another delivery to my boy's place tonight as well, but now I'm questioning the wisdom of it. It's likely a bit much for a first date gift. But the idea has itched at my brain for the past two weeks, and I couldn't resist.

I pace in my dining room, anxiously waiting for food to arrive, but more so waiting for a text from my boy with a reaction to his gift. *My boy...* It has such a nice ring to it, but I'm still not sure it's true. Not quite yet anyway. We're on a path, and tonight's date, even virtual, is a step in the right direction.

My phone vibrates at the same time my doorbell rings. I hustle to answer the door while pulling out my phone at the same time. The text I have waiting for me from BraveBoy has a light sweat breaking out over my skin. I know he wanted to use fake names, but I saved his number under BraveBoy anyway. I don't want to settle for another name that isn't his. I'll wait as long as I have to for the real thing.

BraveBoy: I got the gift you sent...

I thank the delivery man, snatching the bag of food and using one thumb to type a response.

Daddy: What do you think?
BraveBoy: You're naughty, Daddy.

He tacks on a little devil emoji, and I grin in relief.

Daddy: You mentioned that you've been struggling to have a satisfying solo workout. I thought this might help.

BraveBoy: I've never used one before, but I have this fantasy...

I groan, setting the bag of food down on my dining room table and palming my hardening cock through the soft fabric of my suit pants.

Daddy: I want to hear ALL about that. But first, did your dinner arrive?

A picture of open Styrofoam containers comes through in response. I frown, taking a second to unpack my own food and transfer it onto a plate, then I send a reply.

Daddy: This is a date. We may not be in the same place tonight, but we can make it nice by being civilized and putting our food on plates, at least.

I attach a picture of my own food to demonstrate. It takes a few minutes before a response comes through.

BraveBoy: You're right. I'm sorry, Daddy.

A picture follows of the food now on a plate. I can see in the edge of the picture that he seems to have dressed up like I did, a pair of black slacks at the bottom of the frame.

Daddy: Show me what you wore for our first date.

An image comes through a minute later.

He *is* dressed for our date in a pair of black slacks and a white button-up shirt. He looks petite, the kind of boy I could tuck under my arm, close to my chest, when we're out at an event, or curl around tightly in bed at night. His neck is long and slim, begging for mouth-shaped bruises and maybe one day a collar? I know I'm getting ahead of myself.

I send through a picture as well so he can see we had the same idea of dressing up, even if we're not in the same place. Although, I *am* more casual than I would be if we were out somewhere. I skipped the tie, and my top couple of buttons are open, tufts of auburn chest hair peeking out as well as the barest hint of a tattoo that I got during my wild, rebellious youth.

BraveBoy: You look better than dinner, Daddy.

Daddy: I was just thinking the same about you. If you were here, I'd plan to have you for dessert, spread out on the table and topped with whipped cream… Something to look forward to another time.

BraveBoy: Daddy…

I chuckle, hearing the groan even in the black and white words on the screen. I meant to tease *him*, but my cock is achingly hard at the image I just painted. *Patience*.

As much as I want to circle back to his comment about the fantasy, this *is* a date, and a little civilized conversation is called for while we eat. In perfect first date form, we end up discussing our childhoods. He tells me all about being raised by his grandfather, who recently passed, and I regale him with stories of my mild rebellions and the grief I gave my mother.

It's easy to forget our entire date is taking place over text message, a relaxed smile on my lips the entire time. The biggest downside is how much I'm aching to reach out and touch him, find out if this connection we seem to have is real.

When our plates are clean, I get up to tidy up and then retire to my living room, my phone still close at hand. I settle myself on the couch, undoing a few more buttons on my shirt and running a hand over the half-hard bulge in the front of my pants, groaning at the twitch of my cock against my palm.

Daddy: So, about that fantasy you mentioned earlier...

It takes a few seconds for him to respond, and I wonder if I'm pushing too far, too fast. It's one thing to flirt a bit; it's another to explicitly discuss sex, especially in light of the present I sent for him.

BraveBoy: I'm blushing so hard right now.

I hum, imagining the pale skin on his chest pinked up with nervous arousal. If he were here with me right now, I'd pull him onto my lap and chase the heated path of his blush with my lips, playing with him until he's so turned on he forgets his nerves and tells me exactly how I can make all of his fantasies come true.

BraveBoy: If we were in person, I'd never manage to say this aloud.

Daddy: If we were in person, I would make sure you forgot all about being anxious or embarrassed.

BraveBoy: How?

Daddy: I'd pull you onto my lap, and you'd feel how hard I already am for you. Then I'd kiss you and whisper sweet, dirty things into your ear until you're horny and squirming, dying to tell me all your naughty fantasies and wet dreams.

BraveBoy: Ungh. I AM horny and squirming.

Groaning, I unbutton my pants and slide my hand inside to palm my hot, throbbing erection.

On impulse, I snap a picture, not of my cock, but of my tented pants, bulging with my hand inside, wrapped around my cock, my knuckles stretching the fabric and a messy tangle of fiery pubes peeking out.

I send the image to him, and the response is a long string of random letters and numbers, followed by a second, coherent text.

BraveBoy: Oh my god, I think you just broke

my brain. That's the hottest thing I've seen in my entire life. I wish I was kneeling between your legs right now, watching you touch yourself.

Daddy: Something to look forward to another time…

Daddy: Now, be a good boy and tell Daddy your fantasy about the toy I sent.

BraveBoy: In my fantasy, I have a vibrating plug like this in, nestled against my prostate, keeping me hard and horny while I'm at a party. But I lose the controller for it, and the man I have a crush on finds it. He follows me somewhere private and uses the controller to make me come over and over until I can't take it anymore, forcing orgasm after orgasm, ringing me out until my cock is sensitive and my balls are throbbing and empty. Then, he scoops me up off the floor, where I'm breathless and drenched in my own cum, and kisses me all over, making me melt in his arms, all floaty and happy.

It's all too easy to imagine the scenario he's describing, the image of it sending desperate pulses through my cock. I tighten my grasp around my base, heat flaring in the pit of my stomach and dancing through me.

Daddy: Oh, you ARE a dirty boy.

BraveBoy: Sorry…

Daddy: It wasn't a complaint, sweet boy.

I stroke my cock slowly for a minute, teasing myself while I contemplate whether what I'm about to say will be too much too fast. I suppose there's only one way to find out.

Daddy: The one I sent you came with an app. All you would have to do is tell me the code inside the box, and I can sync my phone to it.

BraveBoy: Oh my god, Daddy. I'm so hard right now I'm literally dripping precum.

A few seconds later, a picture comes through to prove his point. His cock is a work of art, short and thick, the head deep red with a clear string of precum hanging off the tip. My mouth waters at the sight of it, another throbbing pulse ricocheting from my balls all the way to the tip of my cock.

Daddy: We can play, Brave Boy, but you're going to need a safeword first.

Emerson

A low whine trembles out of my throat. A safeword? That makes this so much more real. I need a safeword because a *Daddy* wants to play with me. *My* Daddy? It's starting to feel that way, but I don't want to get ahead of myself.

My hand has been wrapped around my cock since we started dirty texting right after dinner. It was all I could do to put my used dishes in the sink and get back to the couch to shove my pants down and touch myself. I've been hard since I found the present on my doorstep when I got home from work. I'm not sure why I never thought to buy one for myself, considering the vivid fantasies I've had about using one, but it's so much more special to know it came from him.

I take a moment to consider his request. This time we're only texting, but I should choose a safeword I know I'll be able to say reliably. A shiver of excitement runs through me at the thought of meeting him in person one day, playing with him in real life, and feeling his big, strong hands all over me.

BraveBoy: Unicorn

It takes longer than I would've expected for Daddy to respond. Did he change his mind about playing?

Daddy: Unicorn it is.

I breathe a sigh of relief at his response.

Daddy: Now, why don't you get your new toy out, and we can have some fun together.

I manage to pry my hand off my cock and grab the box to open it. I don't know how Daddy knew, but it's absolutely perfect: purple and sparkly, long enough that it will likely hit my prostate, and thin enough to be comfortable but still make me feel nice and full. My cock jerks and my balls tighten as I run my fingers along the smooth, rounded edge of the plug.

I was up late last night, shamelessly jerking off to Alton Brown on *Iron Chef*—don't judge, we all have our guilty pleasures—so, luckily, I have a bottle of lube already handy here in the living room.

I text Daddy the code he needs to sync his app to my toy and then lube up my fingers to get myself ready. Something feels wrong about this though. Not wrong as in I don't want to do it, but wrong as in it's not enough. I want him to tell me what to do, to be in charge of every step, to be the one to make me come, even if it's only my own hands on me this time. But I'm so trembly right now, there's no way I'll be able to avoid stuttering if I have to talk to him. I don't want him to know...not yet. He thinks I'm so perfect right now; I'm not ready to ruin it by becoming someone he pities.

He *did* say he loves pleasing his boy, and right now, that's me. Maybe I can just ask for what I want?

BraveBoy: I need something, Daddy.

Daddy: Tell me.

BraveBoy: I need your voice. I want to hear you telling me what to do, how to finger myself open and when to touch myself. But...I'm not ready to talk. Is that okay?

Daddy: Anything you need, I'll give it to you. You want me to call and do all the talking?

BraveBoy: Yes.

The phone rings with a call almost immediately. I answer with my lube-free hand and make a small, needy noise so he knows I'm here.

"Hey there, my brave, sweet boy." His voice is a deep, gravelly growl. Something about it is familiar, but I can't put my finger on it exactly. It's like I've heard it before, but maybe that was only in a dream. "Are you ready to play?"

"Mmhmm," I hum, putting the phone on speaker and setting it down next to me on the couch so I can use both hands to reach between my legs, not touching anything fun yet since Daddy hasn't told me to.

"I don't want the plug to hurt your pretty little hole, so let's get you nice and stretched first. I want you to slide two lubed fingers between your cheeks and tease your hole for me."

I let out a breathy sound, propping my legs up on the coffee table and spreading them wide, and then gently teasing the rim of my hole with the slick tips of two fingers.

"I bet your hole is hot, isn't it?" The question doesn't seem to require an answer because he keeps talking without pause. "Your fingers probably fit so snug in there, making you shake and moan, desperate for something bigger to fill you."

I press harder against my softening pucker, wanting to slip my fingers inside just like he's describing, but he hasn't told me to yet, so I continue to tease, petting and stroking myself until I'm soft and slick and so, *so* ready for more.

"Push those fingers inside, sweetheart. Open yourself up so Daddy can make you scream later."

A shaky moan falls from my lips as I push both fingers inside easily, the burn of the stretch only lasting for a second before it's not enough. My cock twitches against my belly, hard and still dripping precum, my balls tight and aching as I fuck myself slowly, spreading the lube inside and out. I can hear his panting breaths through the phone. I want to ask if he's touching himself, but I'm too afraid to ruin the moment with my clumsy words.

I cant my hips, fucking myself with my fingers and making wild, desperate sounds until Daddy's voice rumbles through the phone again.

"Stop."

I still at his command, my fingers shoved

deep inside, my last knuckle pressed hard against my rim.

"It sounds like it's time for your plug. Go ahead and get it nice and slick, and then put just the tip inside yourself. No deeper than the tip, got it?"

"Mmhmm," I hum again, reaching for the lube and the pretty plug to do as he says. Once it's nice and slippery, I spread my legs wider and notch it against my relaxed, ready hole, easing just the tip inside. My inner muscles flutter and clench, desperate for more. If I were alone, I'd probably shove it all the way in at once, but I have to admit, the anticipation *is* making it a little more exciting. Daddies are so smart.

"Feels nice, doesn't it?" he purrs again, not seeming to require an answer. "That first inch, that's where most of your nerve endings are. Well, except for that sweet bundle deep inside, but we'll get to that in due time. First…"

The toy vibrates to life, and I let out a startled sound that quickly turns into a moan, the sensation lighting up every one of the million nerve endings around my rim. My toes curl, and my balls squeeze tighter.

"Ungh," I grunt as my cock spills another burst of precum onto my skin.

"Just another inch, nice and slow," he instructs, and I push the toy a little deeper, careful not to let my horny greed get the best of me. I want to feel it all, every smooth, vibrating inch of it filling me. Even better, I wish it was his cock, hot and pulsing with arousal, filling me up.

I could've sworn the plug was only four or five inches long, but it seems to take an eternity to get it all the way inside with the way he insists I do it little by little. The vibrations are even more intense against the outside of my hole as the shape flares wider, stretching me as I ease it inside. My thighs tremble and sweat starts to bead on my skin. Every inch of my body feels electrified and sensitive, my cock so desperate for touch I can hardly keep myself from reaching for it.

"Oh, sweetheart, those desperate, raspy sounds you're making are driving me out of my mind," he rumbles. "I wish I could see how you look, trembling and horny, writhing for me."

"Ungh," I groan again, seating the plug fully into place and feeling the slow vibration against my prostate.

"Does it fit just right? Is it hitting that perfect bundle of nerves inside of you?" he asks, again not waiting for an answer. "Let's find out."

In the next breath, the vibrations intensify, going from slow and gentle to a faster pulse, bursts of sensation directly against my prostate, making my cock leak like a waterfall.

"Ahh," I cry out, grabbing fistfuls of the couch cushions to keep from touching my cock, but unable to stop myself from humping up into the air.

"Sounds like it's just right," Daddy says, sounding satisfied. "There are so many different vibration patterns, we might just have to try them all out."

The vibration changes again. This time each vibration lasts several seconds before stopping and then repeating. The short interval without vibration is almost more intense than the pulsing itself, my breath catching each time, my inner muscles clenching as I wait for the vibrations to start up again.

"How's this one, sweet boy?" He tries another pattern, this one three quick pulses followed by a long one, and then nothing before starting over. My back arches involuntarily, noises I can't even describe bursting out of my mouth as I shake from head to toe, thrashing and nearly sobbing. "I've never heard such beautiful sounds." His voice sounds strained. Is he right on the edge too?

Heat starts to pool in the pit of my stomach, my balls so tight I know I'm going to come any second, even without touching my cock. "Daddy," I grit out between clenched teeth.

"Come, naughty boy. Come for Daddy."

I cry out in relief and ecstasy, his permission unleashing a wave that rushes through my body, sweeping me away as my inner muscles start to clench and throb around the toy, my cock giving another jerk against my belly before spilling hot, sticky ropes of my release all over my skin, shooting up to land on my chest, my throat, even my chin.

But he doesn't let up with the vibration. Even as my prostate and cock become sensitive, he increases the speed of the vibration, not giving me a second to rest. My muscles tense and relax, waves of aftershocks turning into a fresh crest of arousal, another orgasm hot on the heels of the first.

"Oh, oh, oh," I pant.

"Give Daddy another one," he growls, his voice tight and almost choked like he's hanging on by a thin thread.

This time, my cum dribbles out, running down my over-sensitive cock and creating a cascade of sensations, the hot, wet feeling almost too much to bear. My blood is rushing so loudly in my ears I just barely hear an animalistic roar through the phone, the sound of Daddy getting off too. Somehow, that brings a fresh wave of rapture. Daddy's pleasure is my pleasure, and it's a fucking breathtaking thing.

"Such a good boy," he groans. "Sweet, perfect boy." He murmurs more nice things, but most of them get lost in the buzzing inside my ears.

As my second orgasm fades, the vibrations against my prostate are too much, bringing tears to my eyes and my safeword to my lips. But Daddy knows. Even miles and miles away, he knows it's enough before I can even tell him.

The vibrations cease so suddenly it almost feels like I'm missing a step. I let out another shocked cry, my whole body sagging with relief.

We're both quiet for a while, until I start to wonder if he hung up after he turned off the plug. I manage to gather the energy to reach for my phone with my clean hand, and find the call still connected.

I want to say something to him, thank him for the best orgasm…well, *orgasms*, of my life. But my brain is too sluggish, and my body feels too heavy to say a word, so instead I just sigh happily into the phone, and a warm chuckle is the answer I get.

"Thank you for tonight," he says in nearly a whisper. "I'm sorry I'm not there to hold you right now, but it's something to look forward to."

He's said that several times tonight, leaving no room for me to question whether he's interested in more than this. The question is, am I brave enough?

I hold the phone against my chest, imagining he can hear my heartbeat, and then I press a kiss to the screen.

"Night," I whisper before hitting the button to end the call.

CHAPTER 8

Kiernan

I've been half-hard all day, replaying last night over and over. As unbelievably erotic as the whole thing was, there's one word I've been stuck on. *Unicorn*. What are the odds? He only said two words on the phone, so it was impossible to tell if it *was* Emerson, or if I just wanted it to be.

The line at the coffee shop moves forward, and I absently follow it, still lost in the same thoughts I've been lost in all day. The biggest question is, if it *is* Emerson, does that change anything? The boy isn't ready to share his identity, and I want to respect that. Which means I'm going to have to choose not to care whether it's him or not. I'll know the answer eventually. Whoever BraveBoy is, he's mine now, and I'll be as patient as I have to. He can have all the time he needs to become comfortable and ready to meet in person. Until then, I can think of a few more gifts he might like to receive.

The line moves again, and it's my turn to order. I request an iced coffee and move aside to wait for it to be ready. As soon as I'm out of the line, I notice the very man who's been occupying my thoughts today. Emerson is at the back of the line, studying the menu hanging on the wall with a cute furrow between his eyebrows.

"Having trouble deciding?" I ask, inadvertently startling a jump out of him.

"T-t-trying to convince m-myself n-not to have caffeine this l-l-l-late in the day," he confesses with a sweetly crooked smile. That's possibly the greatest number of words he's ever spoken to me in a row. And he's not even blushing or trembling. Either I've lost my touch, or he's decided he's no longer terrified of me. Whatever has brought on this new bout of confidence, I'll take it.

"Mm, no, caffeine this late in the day isn't ideal. It will keep you up all night. Why don't you get a frappe with a lot of whipped cream and enjoy a nice sugar rush instead?" I suggest, in part curious about what his reaction will be to the hint of authority I infuse my voice with.

His cheeks *do* pink this time, but it's still very different from the nervous blush I'm used to seeing. Emerson licks his lips and gives a quick nod. "Okay," he agrees, and I practically purr with satisfaction.

With that decision made, he eyes the pastry case and his stomach growls loudly. Emerson laughs, putting a hand over his stomach and giving me a sheepish look.

"Skipped lunch?" I guess.

"The shop w-w-was b-busy."

I narrow my eyes at the pastry case in question. It's past five o'clock, which means he didn't have lunch, and he's considering a blueberry muffin for his dinner. There's no doubt in my mind that it will bother me all night if I let it stand.

"Let me take you to dinner."

His eyes widen, and it looks like he holds his breath for several excruciating seconds while my own doubts fill my mind. If Emerson *isn't* BraveBoy—and he very well may not be—am I betraying my boy?

"As friends," I tack on, both to reassure him and to ease my own sense of guilt.

"Um..." He shoves his hand into his pocket like he's reaching for his phone, and my heart beats faster. Maybe he has the urge to check in with someone? Perhaps a certain *LonelyDaddy*? He seems to think for a few seconds before finally giving another sharp nod. "Okay."

I can't stop the smile from spreading across my face. "Great. Let's go." I tilt my head toward the door, unconcerned about my abandoned iced coffee as I lead Emerson out of the cafe, a gentle hand between his shoulder blades.

My car is parked just down the block, and when we reach it, I open the passenger door for him and guide him inside.

"W-where are we g-g-going?" he asks once I join him in the car.

"Where would you like to go?" I'm more than happy to make a decision on the matter, but I'd rather know what he likes first.

"N-N-Nothing with food I c-can't pronounce," he answers, wrinkling his nose and drawing a laugh from me.

"How's your Italian?" I tease.

"Linguini, f-fettucine, s-s-ss-spaghetti," he replies.

"Perfection." I grin and pull out of the parking spot, set on taking him to my favorite Italian bistro.

Inside the restaurant, the hostess greets me with a familiar smile. "Your usual table?" she asks.

I give Emerson a wry smile. "I come here a lot," I explain needlessly. "My usual is fine," I tell Maria, and she grabs a couple of menus and leads us to a nice little table right near the large window, looking out at the busy street. It's perfect for people-watching when I come here alone to eat, which is often.

I pull out his chair and then take my own seat, not bothering to look at the menu. Instead I study Emerson as he looks over the options, the furrow returning between his eyebrows. I'm half tempted to pull out my phone and send a message to BraveBoy, just to see if Emerson's phone chimes, but I can't bring myself to do it. I promised myself I'd give him time to come around on his own and tricking him into revealing the truth is the opposite of that.

"Everything l-l-looks good. I c-can't decide," he says, lowering the menu and looking across the table at me.

"Would you like me to order for you?"

His lips twitch, and he bobs his head eagerly.

The waiter appears, and I place my order for eggplant parmesan for myself and seafood linguini for Em as well as a bottle of wine.

"Thank you," he says softly after the waiter leaves.

"It's my pleasure. Tell me, Emerson, how was your day?"

He seems to consider the question for a moment, taking a sip of his water and laying his napkin over his lap before answering. "L-l-ll-long."

I chuckle. "Mine as well. It's lovely to share a dinner with good company after such a tedious day."

This time it's Emerson who laughs, reaching for the glass of wine the waiter just returned to pour for each of us. "I'm n-not sure I q-qualify as good company."

"Why would you think that?" I take a sip from my own glass, patiently waiting while he appears to get his thoughts in order, a number of expressions flitting over his face before he shakes his head quickly. "Because you don't talk much?" I guess, and he shrugs, letting me know that's exactly what he meant by it. "Emerson, my dear boy, there are too many people in the world who talk a lot and don't say a damn thing worth listening to. You make every word count."

His cheeks pink, and there's no mistaking the pleased look that graces his face this time. "T-t-that's a nice thing to s-s-ss-say."

"It's true. Now, tell me what you've been reading lately."

The question seems to loosen him up, and he launches into telling me all about a sci-fi series that has captured his attention. We spend the rest of the meal discussing books and the terrible movies that have bastardized them. The longer the conversation goes on, the more relaxed

Emerson appears to be, speaking for extended lengths of time and stuttering less. If I didn't have a crush on him before this, the passionate way he discusses the twisted perception that *Wuthering Heights* is a love story would certainly have done it for me.

"Wow. Look at the time," I note as we finish off our shared dessert of tiramisu.

"Oh." He blushes again, checking the time himself. Something that looks like guilt passes behind his eyes, and the wall that's come down over the past couple of hours goes back up right before my eyes. "I c-can't believe I talked s-s-s-so long."

"It was a lovely evening with a new friend," I say, reaching for the bill at the same time Emerson slides his hand over to grab it. "I'll take care of it."

"If it's n-n-n-not a date, th-th-th-then I should p-p-pp-pay for myself." He stammers out the argument, one hand clutched around the leather billfold. He's nervous. A few hours just the two of us and I'm already starting to see the signs.

"I invited you, and when I invite a friend out for a meal, I always pay," I lie. Not that I *wouldn't* if Barrett or Alden would allow such a thing. Whatever the cost of the meal, it's inconsequential to me.

Emerson gives me a skeptical look, staring me down defiantly until my cock starts to stir. Oh, he has a fiery side underneath all of the sugary sweetness. I do love that.

"F-f-fine, but I'll p-pay next t-time."

I smirk, knowing full well I'll never allow that to happen. But we can cross that bridge when we get there. "Deal."

He releases his grip, and I slide my Black Card inside and hand it to the waiter as he passes.

Once we're all paid up, I stand and offer Emerson a hand to help him up as well.

"I'd better get you home."

"B-back to my car," he corrects.

"You had three glasses of wine," I say, leaving no room for argument with my tone. "I'll have your car brought to your place."

I half expect another flash of defiance, but he doesn't resist, simply lets me lead him back out to the car, leaning into my touch just the barest amount while we walk.

CHAPTER 9

Emerson

I fidget in my seat as Kiernan pulls into the parking lot of my apartment complex. In spite of his use of the word *friends* at both the beginning and the end of the evening, the squirmy, guilty feeling in my stomach keeps telling me that this was suspiciously like a date. It's not helping that he's been acting incredibly weird since I told him where I live. He's been gripping the steering wheel like his life depends on it and darting glances at me out of the corner of his eye the entire drive to my place.

I clear my throat, trying to work out what I should say. Maybe I shouldn't say anything? I could just get out of the car and sprint upstairs where I can crawl into bed and pretend this awkward, guilt-inducing evening didn't happen. Except...it wasn't *all* awkward, and that kind of makes it worse.

The sound of my clearing throat seems to snap him out of whatever thoughts he's been lost in since we left the restaurant. He turns his head, looking me up and down in a meaningful way.

"Thank you for letting me feed you. Your growling stomach would've been on my mind the rest of the night otherwise."

Fuck if he isn't sweet. It was only a simple meal, but I feel like I've had a taste of what it'd really be like to have the full attention of a Daddy. The way he was constantly keeping an eye out to make sure I was enjoying myself, choosing the perfect meal, pulling out my chair, insisting on paying…it was all so *perfect*. Of course that only adds to my guilt.

"Thank *you*." My fingers flex against the door handle while I try to work out what else to say, what else I *should* say.

It looks like he's considering the same question, an array of emotions passing over his face, his mouth opening and closing several times before he lets out a long breath and finally speaks again.

"Go in and get some sleep," Kiernan says in a gentle yet commanding voice, and I try to hide the shiver it sends down my spine. There's something in the low timbre of his voice that itches at the back of my mind, but I can't put a finger on what it is. Maybe it's nothing more than the wine going to my head.

"Night," I say softly before slipping out of

the car and heading straight for the door to the building. I can hear Kiernan's car idling, waiting until I'm inside. I jog up the steps to my apartment and flick on the light as soon as I step inside.

I kick off my shoes and go to the window, peeking out to see Kiernan's car still sitting down there. It's too far to see the man himself, but I wonder if he sees me because once I pull back the curtain, the car finally leaves. Was he waiting to make sure I got into my apartment okay? Another happy thrill goes through me at the idea, but it mixes with the guilt and makes my stomach churn.

I pace around my living room for several minutes, trying to decide what to do, before I finally pull out my phone and send a text to Daddy.

BraveBoy: I did something, and I'm afraid you're going to be mad…

The text doesn't show as read right away, so I jump onto the M4M app to see if he's active. There's no green dot next to his name. He must be busy. I stare at my phone, simply waiting for a few minutes before deciding to get in the shower to take my mind off of worrying until he messages me back.

The hot spray of the water feels like heaven on my tired body. It really was a long, exhausting day. I had a big shipment of books today, and a popular author just released a new book in their bestselling series, which meant the store was slammed.

I suds up my body with a vanilla scented bar of soap, trying hard not to think about how sweet Kiernan was tonight and how much easier it was to talk to him than it usually is. It was easier to talk to him because sex with Daddy last night gave me heaps of new confidence. We might not have been in the same room, but we had sex…and then I betrayed him by letting Kiernan take me out for dinner.

My eyes burn with unshed tears, shame clogging my throat as I hurry through the rest of my shower. By the time I get out, my phone is blinking with a new message. My hand trembles as I reach for it, the other clutching the towel I have wrapped around my waist.

Daddy: Tell Daddy and I'll decide if I'm mad.

BraveBoy: There's this man, a friend of a

friend really, he's a Daddy too…

Daddy: What happened?

BraveBoy: Nothing. He just took me to dinner.

It sounds so innocent when I write it out like that. Maybe I need to give him more context, like the crush I've had for months or how nice it was to let Kiernan take care of me tonight.

Little dots pop up to show he's typing before disappearing again. This happens several times while my stomach twists itself in knots. Is he so mad he doesn't even know what to say? Is he trying to decide how to tell me we shouldn't talk anymore?

I clutch my phone close, wandering into my bedroom and dropping my damp towel next to the bed before climbing in and pulling my blanket up over my head. There's a sense of safety in my makeshift blanket fort. I pull my knees up to my chest and stare intently at my phone until a message finally appears, sending my heart into a wild flail. I clench my eyes closed before reading it, telling myself that whatever he said, it's not the end of the world.

Kiernan

As soon as Emerson told me his address, any doubt I had that he and BraveBoy were one and the same was completely obliterated. How I managed to hold it together in that moment is a mystery to me. And now, here he is, guiltily confessing to going to dinner with me.

My hands tremble as I clumsily type a reply —*Sweetheart, it's me*. My finger hovers over the Send button, but I pause. Is this the right way to go? I don't want to be dishonest with him, but maybe the anonymity is what he needs right now in order to explore and learn about himself?

I stroke my fingers thoughtfully through my beard, considering how to handle this. I type and delete several more responses, not entirely confident in any of them. I'm not used to lacking confidence. I can't say I enjoy the feeling. The real question is, what's best for Emerson? It's my job to know that, but I have to admit to myself that in this instance, I don't. The best I can do is to ask.

Daddy: I'm not mad.

Daddy: I need you to help me understand

what you need. If this man is the reason you want to learn more about the lifestyle, then maybe it would be best if you spoke to him. If you're more comfortable with messaging, then maybe reach out through the app or with a text to discuss things with him?

BraveBoy: I'm not ready. And…I like you. I want to get to know you more. I know it's only texting, but I feel a connection when we talk. You're helping me become more confident. I don't want to give you up.

Daddy: You won't have to give me up; I can promise you that.

I bounce my knee and return to thought. If he's not ready to pursue a relationship outside of texting, but he feels that he wants me…*needs* me…then maybe the right thing to do is to let things play out. If the best Daddy I can be to him right now is LonelyDaddy, then I can be that.

Daddy: Here's what we're going to do. Nothing changes until you're ready for it to change. We can keep talking and having virtual dates if you still want them, but I need you to promise me something.

BraveBoy: Yes.

I chuckle at his eagerness, ready to make a promise before he even knows what I'll ask. Such a good boy.

Daddy: Promise me you'll let yourself be open to getting to know your friend. If something develops organically, it's okay. Trust me.

BraveBoy: I do trust you. I promise.

BraveBoy: I have a question though.

Daddy: Yes?

BraveBoy: Can we still have sex?

I laugh again. He may come across as shy and blushing, but Emerson is a dirty boy inside. I love knowing that secret about him. I love that he's saved that for me.

Daddy: If that's what you want.

BraveBoy: It is. Thank you, Daddy. I was so confused and felt so guilty. I should've asked you before agreeing to go with him tonight, and I was so worried you'd never want to talk to me again.

Daddy: It's okay, sweet boy. I WOULD like to know what's going on with you, just so I can make sure you're safe. But I'm not upset, and I'm glad you talked to me about it.

BraveBoy: Thank you. Will you tell me about your day? Or...do you think you could call just so I can hear your voice?

His request lights me up from head to toe before giving me pause. I called last night, but we were both so lust-drunk that he didn't recognize my voice. What if he can tell? I wrestle with the question. I don't want to purposefully hide anything from him and not calling for fear he'll recognize my voice feels like exactly that. I won't come right out and tell him, but I won't purposefully deceive him either. That's the best way I can take care of my boy. And it *is* starting to feel like he's mine. If I don't rush, if I'm as patient as he needs me to be, he might be mine one day.

I hit the button to call, and he answers on the first ring. He doesn't say a word, but I can hear the sound of his breathing through the phone.

"Hey there, my brave sweet boy," I murmur into the phone, kicking off my shoes and lying back on my bed. "My bed is so big and empty. I hope it's okay that I'm imagining you here with me, cuddled up close while we talk about how our days were."

He makes a sound that I take as agreement, or at least that he wants me to keep painting that picture for him. "I love the idea of naked cuddle time right after work before we move on to the rest of our evening. It sounds like a wonderful transition from workday to our time together. You know, I've never had a boy all my own to come home to every night, but I've certainly given the idea a lot of thought."

"Mm," he hums another happy noise, and now that I'm listening for it, I'm convinced I can recognize his voice, even in just that simple sound. Maybe I'm being a bit silly, but it feels like fate that we found each other on the app. Or maybe it just means we're compatible.

"I have an idea, why don't I read to you." I reach for the book that's on my nightstand, a classic I've been trying to get through for my book club. I swear, while I was on a mission to pick something exciting, everyone else is desperate to prove how literary they are. But maybe it will be more enjoyable to read aloud to my boy than it is to read to myself. *"Call me Ishmael,"* I read in a deep timbre.

Emerson makes noises every so often on the other end, letting me know he's still there, and he's listening. And eventually the noises turn to soft snores.

I set the book aside and listen to him breathe for a few minutes before whispering "goodnight" and hanging up the phone.

CHAPTER 10

Emerson

My fingers fly over my keyboard, a dirty grin spread over my lips. All of the sexy chats Daddy and I have had in the past couple of weeks have given me tons of fuel for my erotica stories, and my readers have been eating it up. There's even been some speculation on my social media pages about what could've brought about all the new, *extremely detailed* stories.

I squirm, my cock hardening as the story unfolds on my screen of a boy who gets off on almost getting caught, so he jerks off on his balcony where his next-door neighbor—AKA the Daddy of his dreams—can hear every gasp and moan. I wonder if Daddy would be interested in role playing some of my stories with me—for research purposes, of course.

The alarm on my phone sounds, dragging me out of the story in a jarring way.

"Damn," I mutter, saving the doc and closing my laptop. I should've known better than to get lost in writing when I'm supposed to go to

Sterling's tonight so Nolan can give us all the details on the launch plans for our libraries, and I can update everyone on the book donations we now have rolling in.

I slide off the bed and lazily palm my half-hard cock. Maybe I can get Daddy to call me later for one of our dirty chats. In the meantime, I need to stop playing with my dick and get dressed so I can leave.

While I dig through my dresser, I wonder if Kiernan might stop by the house at all tonight. He's been into the bookstore more and more but hasn't asked me out for another meal. Although sometimes it seems like he *wants* to, like he's torn about it. Maybe he doesn't want to send me the wrong message? Or maybe he's met someone else. The thought is disappointing, even if I'm falling harder for Daddy every day.

I pull out my unicorn shirt and look at it, trying to decide what to do. Daddy said it was okay, that I can get to know Kiernan better. But does that include dressing with the other man in mind?

With a huff, I toss the shirt aside and grab a different one, plain purple this time, completely devoid of mythical horses. I finish getting dressed and then hustle out the door, sending a quick apology to Sterling about running late before getting in my car.

By the time I arrive, Nolan's car is already in the driveway. Sterling greets me at the front door with a smile and a hug, ushering me inside and offering a drink.

"N-no thanks."

Nolan and Gannon are waiting in the living room for us, taking up the loveseat like usual. I notice Nolan brushing his hand against Gannon's arm, trying to make it seem casual, but the way he watches the quiet man makes me think he's trying to get his attention without being too obvious. Silly boy, he should know he already has Gannon's attention.

"S-s-sorry I'm late." I grab a seat and flip open my notebook to where I left off during our last meeting.

"Ain't no problem," Sterling assures me.

"Yeah, we were just gossiping," Nolan agrees, bumping his knee against Gannon's subtly.

"Why don't we start with you," Sterling says, nodding toward me.

"Sure." I launch into telling them all about how successful the social media campaign I've been running is doing and also how willing the other bookstores in the area have been to help. All told, we should have plenty of books to start with, and we can continue to grow our collection from there. "Once we s-start showing up in c-c-communities, it will be even easier t-to get people to donate."

"That's so great. I thought it would be a lot harder than that."

"Nah, you j-j-just need the right m-mmm-messaging."

"You're killing it, Em," Nolan says, sounding both impressed and surprised. Should I be offended by that? He tilts his head like he's studying me, and I try not to squirm. "There's something different about you."

I glance down at myself and run my fingers self-consciously through my short hair. "L-l-like what?"

"Hmm, I'm not sure." He taps his chin, his gaze still fixed on me. "It's like you're more confident or something."

A shaky laugh escapes me. More confident? I highly doubt that. Then again, I've never been exposed to the constant stream of compliments Daddy loves to text me. Maybe they're seeping into my brain and making me more self-assured.

I shrug one shoulder.

"Things going well with your Daddy?" Sterling guesses, and my cheeks heat. He takes that as confirmation. "We should go on a double date."

I fight back another slightly panicky bout of laughter. A double date? I haven't even worked up the courage to meet the man yet. He's been so patient and sweet about it, but that can't hold forever. Eventually, I'll have to step outside of this amazing, happy bubble we've been living in and actually meet the man. But there are so many things that can go wrong once that happens. I'm not ready to gamble what we have yet just to find out what could be.

"Eventually," I agree vaguely.

Sterling sticks his bottom lip out in a pout but doesn't push it. And then we get back to the reason we're all here, discussing the mobile library project.

Kiernan

I pull into Barrett's driveway right behind the man himself, with Alden bringing up the rear in his brand-new Lexus. I'm not sure if the stink of loneliness on Alden and myself was just too much to bear, prompting Barrett to invite us over for dinner, or if he simply misses our company. Not that I can blame him for being so wrapped up in Sterling, but we don't spend nearly as much time together as we all used to.

When I get out of my car, I notice a few extra vehicles in the driveway as well. Barrett frowns, scratching his chin. "Damn, I forgot Sterling was holding a meeting at the house tonight. We'll have to stay out of their hair. Luckily, I bought more than enough food for everyone."

My heart leaps at the prospect of spending some time with Emerson tonight. I've been careful to keep my distance the past few weeks, not wanting to put him in an uncomfortable position or needlessly confuse the poor boy. But surely one dinner among friends won't hurt anything. I can get my Em fix, and he doesn't have to feel guilty about it. It's a win-win.

Alden's eyes linger on the beat-up Toyota that must belong to Nolan, the bumper barely hanging on and a crack in the back windshield. Surely, we pay the man enough to afford a better car than that.

The three of us head up the large steps and into the house. As soon as I'm through the door, the sound of Emerson's laughter echoes down the hallway, stopping me in my tracks immediately. My heart stutters to a stop and then breaks into a gallop. I want to be the reason he makes such a lovely sound. I want it more than I want my next breath. I want it more than I want every dime in my bank account.

"Are you all right?" Barrett asks, eyeing me

with concern.

I drag in a breath, not realizing I was so stunned I forgot to for a minute or so. And then I nod. "I'm fine."

I loosen my tie and run my fingers through my hair, freeing it from the neatly combed state I try to preserve during the workday, and then I follow Barrett into his kitchen. Alden helps himself to pouring the three of us drinks while Barrett lays out ingredients, and I grab a knife and get to work chopping the vegetables he hands me. It's a familiar, peaceful process. We all chat and laugh while we work, the smell of cooking food eventually luring the boys into the kitchen as well.

"I thought we might have kitchen fairies," Sterling teases, crossing the kitchen and letting himself be pulled into Barrett's arms for a kiss.

I glance over and find Emerson lingering in the doorway, casting a shy look in my direction. My eyes drop to his shirt. No unicorn today. Did he not think there was a possibility he'd see me, or did he avoid wearing it on purpose? The thought makes me feel warm and chilled all at once. If he *was* dressing with me in mind before, what does it mean that he's not now? Is this a sign that he's falling for Daddy and putting me out of his mind? And exactly how batshit does it make me to be jealous of myself?

"Swe-" I catch myself just in time before my mouth runs away with me, clearing my throat to hide my awkward stumble. "Emerson."

He snaps his eyes to me and straightens up instantly, causing satisfaction to curl around the pit of my stomach. It takes every ounce of restraint I have not to murmur *good boy*.

"Y-y-yes?" he asks in nearly a whisper.

"Come set the table."

He nods quickly, scurrying into the kitchen to grab a stack of plates. I let my eyes fall on his biteable little ass as he carries them out of the room.

"Kiernan," Barrett says my name in a low rumble, clearly a warning.

"Fuck off," I respond flatly, earning me a single *ha* from Alden in between sips of scotch. By his standards, it might as well have been a full guffaw.

Barrett scowls, but doesn't snap back. Instead he kisses his boy's head and gives him a gentle pat on the ass. "Dinner's almost ready, why don't you help Emerson set the table."

"Yes, Daddy," he says sweetly, flouncing off to grab the silverware.

There's a lovely, familial feeling when we all sit down for dinner a short time later. I position myself right across from Emerson.

Nolan and Sterling keep up most of the chatter throughout the meal, but what they talk about, I couldn't tell you. I'm far too busy being mesmerized by every shape Emerson's lips form and every twitch of his expression, from the shy smiles to the almost rapturous appreciation of the food. He's more enthralling than whatever pretentious movie won the Oscars this year.

Will Emerson and I ever get to have what Barrett and Sterling do? Will he be angry when he finds out that I'm LonelyDaddy? I've been struggling for weeks now about my deception, but with Em not being ready for the next step, I feel like I'm trapped between a rock and a hard place. I can either tell him and force him to deal with the situation before he's ready for the next step, or I can cut off communication all together. Neither of those options are acceptable.

When we finish eating, I slip out onto the large back porch to clear my head. There's a beautiful view of the desert with the mountains in the distance. I take a deep breath and brace my hands against the intricately carved railing.

"Oh, s-s-sss-sorry, I didn't know anyone w-w-was out here."

I look over my shoulder to find Emerson trying to slip back inside. "Wait."

He stops and looks back at me warily. "I s-sss-s..."

"I won't bite," I promise. "Come keep me company for a minute or two."

He tugs his lush bottom lip between his teeth, looking back and forth between me and the house, clearly torn. I hold my breath while I wait for his answer, my heart hammering. There's little doubt that he's smitten with LonelyDaddy, but I need some kind of sign that *I* might actually have a shot with him.

"Okay," he finally says, stepping outside and closing the sliding glass door behind him. He joins me by the railing, leaning against it and taking a deep breath just like I did. "S-s-such a nice view."

"It is," I agree. "You should see my place, it's out in the desert with an infinity pool around the back. The stars overhead at night are absolutely awe-inspiring." I'm not sure if I'm bragging or trying to tempt him. Or perhaps it's simply nervous chatter.

"I bet guys l-l-ll-like that."

Do I detect a hint of jealousy? It's so hard to tell.

"Some," I answer. "But, between you and me, the boys who are particularly smitten with my pool don't often stay long after they've dried off."

Emerson frowns. "They s-s-ss-sound s-s-s-sss..." He stops and licks his lips. "They're idiots."

I chuckle. "That is entirely possible," I agree. "I've been working on finding different boys. Maybe then I won't be quite so lonely." I let the word hang between us, realizing I'm tempting fate. Or maybe I'm hoping Emerson will come to the right conclusion on his own.

He doesn't say anything, just nods and continues to enjoy the view. I'm not sure how long we stand there, shoulder to shoulder, sharing a comfortable silence before Em speaks again.

"Did you not l-l-like the b-b-books I recommended?" he asks, sounding adorably shy.

"What? I loved them. Didn't I tell you that when we shared dinner?" I try to think back. We discussed literature quite at length, I'll be surprised if I didn't mention enjoying the books.

"It's just that y-y-you haven't b-been b-b-bb-back."

My heart swells. Part of me wondered if he noticed or minded that I'd stayed away. I guess I have my answer.

"I've been busy. I'll stop by this week though, so why don't you make a stack of recommendations for me."

"How about j-just one so y-y-you don't stay away s-so long?" he barters, his cheeks turning pink at the same time that he fights a sweet smile.

"Deal."

We head back inside after that, rejoining our friends in the midst of what seems to be an argument between Alden and Nolan about the dilapidated car in the driveway. The pretty twink doesn't seem all that impressed with Alden's concern, and the whole thing has brought a scowl to Gannon's already serious face.

Whatever's going on there, Alden clearly has his work cut out for him.

I make my excuses a short time later, eager to get home and message my boy. He must've had the same thought because there's a text waiting for me as soon as I'm stripped down and in bed.

BraveBoy: I've been thinking about you. Will you call me and tell me about your day? I want to close my eyes and pretend we're together.

My fingers itch to respond that we *can* be

together. All he has to do is say the word, and I'll go straight to his place or send a driver to bring him to mine. But he knows we live in the same city. If he was ready to meet, he would've said it. So I hit the call button and settle against my pillow.

"Hi there, my brave boy," I say into the phone, joy filling me at the happy sigh that I receive in reply. "I hope you're ready to be bored to sleep because my day primarily involved going over contracts."

He chuckles but, of course, doesn't say anything. I take that as tacit agreement, and I launch into a terribly dry recitation of my day spent mainly counting down the hours until I could be home talking with him. I leave out the dinner party for obvious reasons, and before long, his soft, rhythmic breathing alerts me that he's asleep.

"Good night, sweetheart," I whisper before hanging up.

Hopefully, he'll be ready to meet soon. I want him in my arms, in my bed, in my *life*. I just hope like hell that he'll want that too.

CHAPTER 11

Emerson

I trudge up the steps to my apartment, exhausted after another long day preceded by a *very* late night. Unfortunately, last night wasn't even anything particularly fun. I was working on some stuff for the mobile libraries and ended up losing track of time. I yawn and reach into my pocket for my apartment key, stopping short when I see a package leaning against my door.

I bend down to pick it up, turning it over to check the label and make sure it's for me. I can't think of anything I've ordered recently, and the mail carrier has a habit of mixing up apartment numbers.

The name on the package simply reads *Tom* followed by my address. I frown, trying to remember my neighbor's name. I could've sworn it was Alex or something with an A. Who the hell is Tom?

It's a testament to how tired I actually am that it takes me a good minute and a half of standing in the hallway, staring at the package, before I remember that Tom was the name I told Daddy.

A smile jumps to my lips, and I give the box a shake, trying to see if I can guess what's inside. Whatever it is, it thuds heavily against the inside of the box. I feel like a kid on Christmas, eager to tear into it and find out what it might be. But, considering the last present Daddy sent me was a butt plug, I'd better go inside before I open it.

I step inside and kick off my shoes, barely letting the door close behind me before I'm tearing the plain brown paper off the package. The box inside the wrapping is just as non-descript, not giving any hints about what the present is. I bounce impatiently on my toes as I pick at the tape along the edge, *finally* getting it loose and getting the box open.

In my excitement to get it open, I fumble it, spilling an exceptionally large dildo to the floor with an impressive *thunk*.

"Holy sh-shit." My eyes go wide as I stoop to pick it up. It's heavy in my hand, the material silky smooth in between the realistic veins adorning the shaft. I've never seen a more lifelike dildo—from the slight curve near the tip to the way the soft silicone moves under my touch. There's even a thicker inch just below the head that makes it look like an uncircumcised erection.

My own cock hardens, and my hole flutters as I hold this beauty in my hands. My Daddy is so good to me.

Leaving the torn packaging abandoned on the floor in front of my door, I carry my present into my bedroom and sit down on my bed, one hand already on my phone, getting ready to text Daddy. I set the dildo down on my bed and palm my hard cock through my pants, groaning quietly. I eye the dildo again, and something catches my eye. There's a brand name etched small near the base…

Clone-a-Cock.

Does that mean…? My breath catches, and my cock twitches against my hand, a wave of lust rushing through me. I press the call button with my thumb, putting it on speaker and then setting it on my bed so I can unbutton my pants.

"Did you get your present?" Daddy asks in a rich, deep voice.

"Mmhmm," I hum, picking the toy up again and wrapping my fingers around the shaft, stroking it just like I would if it were his real cock. "Is it…?" I whisper, grateful that I'm able to get the two words out.

"A replica of my cock?" He guesses the end of the question. "I hope you don't mind. Imagining you fucking yourself with my cock made me so desperately horny I could hardly breathe." There isn't a hint of shame.

Mind? I huff out an amused sound as I line up the large dildo against my cock and hold both together in my fist. My cock pulses out a burst of precum, my breath catching on a moan just feeling his weighty erection against mine. The only way it could feel better was if it was throbbing with his pulse. His arms around me wouldn't exactly hurt matters either, but one step at a time. I'll be ready eventually, and in the meantime, this *really* was a thoughtful gift.

I hump against the toy, and Daddy groans quietly into the phone. Fuck, it must be so hot hearing nothing but the squeak of my bedsprings and the hitch of my breath. I can only imagine the filthy things he's picturing right now. Is his hand down the front of his pants while he tries to conjure the image of my hole being stretched by his cock?

I squirm and gasp at the thought. I want Daddy to get off watching me fuck myself with the present he sent me. I thrust against the toy a few more times, barely able to control myself. Then I reach for my phone again with shaky hands. He's still on the line, breathing heavily and listening to me play, but there's no way I'm going to be able to get out the words I have for him. So, I type out a clumsy text and send it.

BraveBoy: Can we get on video so you can watch me?

I'm already strategizing where I can set up my phone, so he'll have the best view. He lets out a low moan when he reads my text. I can hear rustling on his end, no doubt taking his pants off.

"I'll call you back on video," Daddy says, his voice sounding strained. I hit the button to end the call and scramble to set up my phone, propping it up and spreading my legs so he has a front-row view. The video chat starts to ring, and I hit the button to accept and then grab the lube and dildo and lie back.

I let my eyes flicker to the screen, curious if I'll get a peek at Daddy's face. But, like me, he has the camera angled down to show off his body instead. His shirt is unbuttoned, the white undershirt beneath it rucked up past his slightly round belly, perfectly dusted with auburn hair, just like in his pictures. His large cock is laying hard against his stomach, looking twice as tempting as the exact replica still clutched in my hand.

"Let me see your fingers stretch that pretty hole of yours," he commands in a deep, rumbly voice.

I fumble to drop the dildo and open the

bottle of lube, squeezing a generous amount onto my fingers and then slipping them between my legs. Daddy makes a low moan of appreciation, his cock twitching. Fuck, I want him here, pinning me down and teasing my hole with his own thick fingers. I just have to be bold enough to ask, and I have no doubt he'd be here. My throat tightens and my pulse races at that thought.

I really want to live up to being the Brave Boy he calls me, but my tongue gets stuck when I try to form the words to ask him to come over.

"Relax, sweetheart," Daddy says in a soothing voice.

It's not until his calm voice washes over me that I realize I was trembling with nerves. I take a deep breath, holding it until my heart rate slows and then letting it out. I do that a few more times until my nerves fade.

"Good boy," he praises, those simple two words going straight to my cock. "Show me how you get your hole ready."

I tilt my head back, letting my eyes flutter closed as I slip two slicked fingers inside slowly. Daddy makes another low, growly noise as I work my fingers in and out. I peel one eye open and catch sight of his hand wrapped around his cock. My own erection throbs, twitching and spilling a long, sticky drip of precum against my skin.

I reach for the dildo and squeeze more lube onto it. No matter how much I finger myself, the toy is so big I'll never be able to prep enough, and I'm not in a particularly patient mood.

"No," Daddy says sternly when I line the toy up with my entrance. I huff but go still. "You're not ready. Put down the toy. I want three fingers."

I clutch the toy tighter and let out an indignant puff through my nose. He's not here; he can't *actually* stop me from pushing the cock inside me and riding it until I come. Will I get a punishment if I do? The thought is both exciting and a little intimidating. I'm not sure I'm the disobedient, bratty kind of boy because the memory of the words *good boy* from just a few minutes ago is enough to convince me to do as he says.

I set the toy back down and work two fingers back inside my tight, hot hole, fucking myself a few times before adding a third.

I whine at the sting of the stretch. Okay, fine, he was totally right that I wasn't ready for the girth of the cock yet. I watch the up and down motion of his hand on his cock, and I try to match the rhythm, working my fingers in and out as deep as I can until my inner muscles are relaxed and my balls are tight and aching for release.

I want to beg him to let me use the cock now, to promise him I'm ready for it. I don't even care right now that my words will likely get tangled up around my lips and tongue or what he'll think of me if they do. But Daddy reads my mind like he always seems to. He knows what I need before I even have the chance to tell him.

"Go ahead, but take it nice and slow."

I let out a shaky breath, pulling my fingers out and lining the dildo up a second time. "*Slow*," he says again, the commanding edge in his voice almost enough to make me come all on its own.

Kiernan

I tighten my hand around the base of my throbbing cock to keep myself from coming as I watch Emerson slide the long, thick replica of my cock into his glistening hole. His slim thighs, dusted with dark hair, frame either side of the camera, his heavy balls pulled tight against his body, his cock leaking against his belly, and I stroke myself slowly.

I'm playing with fire if I don't want to finish too soon, but I can't help myself. The needy twitch of his hips, accompanied by the breathy sounds falling from his mouth, is beyond addicting. I wonder how opposed the boy would be to spending a week in my bed, naked and perpetually covered in a mixture of our cum. I may have to propose it after we've met. I can't imagine any amount of my sweet, perfect boy would be enough to sate the craving I have for him.

His thighs tense and tremble, his cock jerking against his stomach as he pushes the toy all the way up to the flared base.

"Ooh," he moans, his hand flying to his cock. It jumps to my lips to tell him to slow down, but my own cock is leaking and my balls are aching.

"I love your pretty cock," I praise, working my hand faster up and down my length, and he does the same, rocking his hips while he pants and whines. If he weren't so worried about me hearing his stutter, would he babble dirty things for me? In the future, will he let me coax them out of him? I want to hear filthy words on his sweet lips, and I want to hear them when his ass is squeezing my cock.

"I want to fuck you deep until you feel me in you for days," I groan. "I want to leave you dripping with my cum."

He moans, his abs tightening and his muscles twitching. He strokes himself even faster, humping into his hand. By the sounds he's making, I'd guess the dildo is sitting just right inside too, grinding against his prostate with every swivel of his hips. I'd give anything to lick the stray droplet of sweat off his skin as it trickles down his chest or to sink my fingers into his slim hips and fuck him nice and deep until he falls apart.

Emerson makes a strangled sound, and his cock starts to pulse, pumping thick ropes of cum over his knuckles and all over his stomach. I slam my hips up, fucking into my fist until the heat in my gut explodes as well, rushing through me as my balls tighten and I make a mess of myself with my release.

I work my hand up and down my cock until Emerson's body relaxes, and he stops stroking himself.

As hard as I just came into my own hand, I'm not feeling all that settled or relaxed, no doubt because I can't tug my boy into my arms and feel his breathing slow as his body softens into a boneless sleep.

I wipe my cum-covered hand on my bamboo sheets and sigh. The camera jiggles on his end and then goes black. A few seconds later, my phone buzzes with a text.

BraveBoy: Was that okay?

Daddy: It was perfect. YOU'RE perfect. I just wish you were in my bed right now instead of across town.

I've been careful not to pressure him, and I don't want to think I am now. But I can't deny how badly I want to be with him.

BraveBoy: I'll be brave enough soon, Daddy. I promise.

Daddy: I'll be here when you're ready

There's no doubt in my mind about that. I'll wait for Emerson as long as I have to, as long as he needs me to. He's worth it.

CHAPTER 12

Kiernan

I absently drag my index finger over the embossed lettering of the invitation that I've been staring at for a solid ten minutes. Boyd's yearly masquerade parties are legendary among the wealthy and connected here in Las Vegas. They tend to be a rather fun time as well.

Last year, an extremely famous pop star was there. Sweet girl.

The question isn't whether I'm going to RSVP to the party, it's whether I'll RSVP with a plus one. Taking anyone other than Emerson is absolutely out of the question. But is my boy ready for a little push, or is it best if I continue to let him set the pace? I hum thoughtfully under my breath, stroking my beard with my free hand.

"Trying to decide which one of the many adoring boys you're going to grace with a request to be your plus one?" Barrett asks. I look up to find him standing in the doorway to my office. "I knocked, but you didn't say anything," he explains.

I wave him in and set the invitation down.

"Not exactly," I answer his question as he settles himself into the chair in front of my desk, crossing his ankle over his knee. I eye my life-long friend. Wanting to let Em set the pace and get comfortable is only part of the problem. I don't *need* Barrett's permission to pursue things, but it will sure as hell make my life a lot easier if he's not all surly and disapproving about the whole thing.

"Why the conflicted expression then?"

"What if I were to ask Emerson to be my date?" I come right out with it. There's no point in playing coy about the issue.

He frowns. "I'm not your keeper."

"You told me to back off," I remind him.

"And I still think you should," he says simply. "I don't think the two of you are a match."

"You're wrong." My voice comes out in an unintended low growl. It's not his fault he doesn't know a damn thing about what's going on, and I don't intend to enlighten him, but he couldn't be more off the mark on this one.

He cocks his head and studies me curiously. "You're already seeing him."

"Not exactly."

"Fine, it's none of my business. But I'll feel a lot better if you make it *abundantly* clear to him that the money this company is investing in the mobile library project is in no way contingent on him reciprocating your interest."

"I'm a lawyer," I remind him.

"Right." He nods. "So, are you going to ask him to the masquerade?"

"I haven't decided." Although knowing that Barrett won't pitch a fit does help tip the scales a bit. I just don't want to rush anything and scare him off. "I think I will take a break for lunch though." That decided, I stand up and button my suit jacket.

He gives me a knowing smirk. "Going to the bookstore?"

"Reading is important," I answer, returning his grin and patting him on the shoulder as I stride past and exit my office.

The afternoon traffic is light, so it doesn't take me long to get to Unicorn Books. I stride into the shop with a spring in my step, intent on reminding Emerson that he promised me a new book recommendation or two.

My boy is behind the front counter, leaning over it and yawning widely. He looks absolutely dead on his feet with dark circles under his eyes and a weary set of his shoulders.

All thoughts of books and flirting fly immediately out of my mind as I approach the counter with concern. "Emerson." I say his name in a firm but gentle tone. He startles, standing up straight immediately and shaking himself like he's trying to dispel his fatigue.

"Hi," he practically squeaks the word. "I have a b-b-b-book for you."

I ignore the book he slides in front of me, still focused on the unusual paleness of his skin. "Are you feeling well? You look exhausted."

He blinks at me in what seems to be surprise. "I've had a f-f-few l-ll-late nights."

My frown deepens. I know I haven't kept him up particularly late at all this week. A momentary flair of jealousy makes me wonder if there could be someone else he's chatting with as well, but I bat that away quickly. He's not the type to do something like that.

Instead of worrying about the cause of his lack of sleep, I go into problem-solving mode. I glance around the shop, looking for Sterling.

"Are you working alone today?"

"S-s-s-ss-Sterling will be in at th-th-three."

I check my watch. It's only one o'clock now. My house is entirely too far away.

"How far is it to your place?" I know his address, but I'm not sure of the distance off the top of my head.

"Twenty m-mm-minutes."

"Hm." I stroke my beard again, trying to come up with a solution.

"What?" he asks.

"I'm trying to think of where I can take you for a nap," I tell him, and he scoffs.

"I c-c-c-cc…" He stops and shakes his head quickly.

"I'll watch the store," I explain patiently, when he fails to get the word out and seems to give up in exasperation.

"Kiernan," he says my name with a hint of frustration, and it settles all wrong over me. I want to hear how the word *Daddy* will sound on his lips. Ideally, slightly breathless as he looks up at me through those thick eyelashes of his, all sweet and needy.

Patience, I remind myself.

"No arguments," I say firmly. He'll only waste his energy, and the result will be the same.

Emerson sighs, clearly knowing he's not going to win this one. "There's a c-couch in the b-b-break room." He points in the direction of the back of the store, and I smile. Before I can convince myself it's too much, I round the counter and stoop to hoist him over my shoulder.

He gasps and grabs onto the fabric of my suit, his body draped over me, his ass up in the air, my hand resting securely against his thigh. My cock hardens immediately, but it's the last thing I'm worried about. My boy needs a nap, and I'm going to make sure he gets one.

I'm not exactly sure where I'm going, but I carry him in the direction he pointed until I find an unmarked door near the back of the shop. I step through and flick on the light switch. It's a small break room with a ratty couch along with a table and two chairs. It'll do.

When I set Emerson on his feet, he's all pink cheeks and shy glances. By the way he quickly angles his body away from me, I have no doubt he's as turned on as I am.

"Lie down," I instruct, shrugging off my suit jacket and rolling it up to create a makeshift pillow. Emerson looks at me in disbelief but doesn't argue. He settles himself onto the couch and yawns again. "Get some sleep, and don't worry about the store. I'll take care of things."

He nods slowly, his eyelids already drooping. "Th-thank you."

I want to lean forward and kiss his forehead, but I resist. I'm fully decided now on the matter of the masquerade. My boy needs me. A virtual Daddy isn't enough; he needs someone to make sure he's getting enough sleep, to take care of all the little things he never thinks of. No, he doesn't need *someone*: he needs me…and I need him.

I don't linger, as much as I'd like to stay and make sure he's sleeping soundly. But I made a promise to watch the store, and I can't have customers going un-helped when he's counting on me.

I switch off the light and slip out of the room quietly, leaving my sweet boy to get the rest he needs.

Emerson

I blink awake, groggy but well rested. There are no windows in the small back room, so there's no way of knowing how long I slept or what time of day it is. For all I know a zombie apocalypse broke out while I napped. An image flashes through my mind of Kiernan standing guard outside the door, fighting off the flesh-eating undead, determined to make sure I get some decent rest.

I smile at the thought and drag myself into a sitting position, immediately missing the scent of Kiernan that was surrounding me while I used his suit jacket as a pillow. A small amount of guilt niggles at the pit of my stomach, but Daddy has insisted over and over that it's okay.

I unfold the suit jacket and frown at the wrinkles that formed in it while I slept, not to mention the embarrassing drool spot that I left. Fuck, I'm sure this thing cost as much as the monthly rent on the bookshop. Not that I can't afford to buy him a new jacket. I'm not as well-off as he is, but I'm not exactly hurting either. I just don't go flaunting it around. All I need to be happy is a dozen unicorn T-shirts, the book shop, and a roof over my head. And Daddy, of course. I smile to myself, thinking about Daddy as I slip into the bathroom to wash my face and make sure I don't have total bed head from my nap.

When I slip back out into the store, I find Sterling behind the counter, ringing up a customer.

"Hey there, sleepy head," he greets me once the customer leaves. "Imagine my surprise when I got in an hour ago and found Kiernan helping a customer, with you nowhere to be found." His tone is teasing, but I grimace, not even wanting to guess what he's thinking right about now. Not that it would take a genius to figure out the conclusion he's drawing.

"H-he w-w-was being nice," I defend with a shrug, smoothing my hand over the silky material of the jacket draped over my arm.

"Uh-huh." He's clearly not buying it. But it really is the truth. "He said he'll get his jacket back later."

I nod and glance around fruitlessly for somewhere to hang it before deciding it's already wrinkled anyway and stuffing it under the cash register. After that, I pull out my phone with the intention to text Kiernan to thank him for earlier. Instead, I get sidetracked by a message from Daddy that's waiting for me.

Daddy: Hey there, Brave Boy. There's something I want to ask you…

Daddy: There's an event I was planning to attend this Saturday, and I'm sorely in need of a date.

My heart thunders at the implication of what he's saying. He's been patient, more than patient. We've been chatting for over a month now. There's no doubt we have a connection, that I trust him, that I'm falling for him, maybe I've already *fallen*. The question is, am I ready to take the risk of meeting him? What if I'm too awkward? What if I get so nervous that I can't get two words out? What if every perfect thing between us is just an illusion?

I nibble on my bottom lip, digging deep to find that well of courage Daddy is so sure I have inside.

It's more than just needing to be brave though. I glance at the suit jacket haphazardly stashed behind the counter. As long as Daddy is a mystery on the other side of a screen, there's a tiny chance he could be Kiernan.

Daddy: It's a masquerade if that helps. You could wear a mask the whole time, protect your secret identity.

A laugh bursts from my lips, calming some of my nerves. He's probably not Kiernan, I've known that from the start, but whoever he is, he's still the caring, patient, extremely sexy Daddy I've been falling for. It's time I finally put aside this crush I have and give him my all.

BraveBoy: I'm not Batman. I'm just…ok, so the thing is, I have a stutter…

Daddy: Okay.

BraveBoy: Like, when I get nervous, I can hardly get my words out. When I'm not so nervous, it's not that bad, maybe just a little annoying to listen to, but you're not going to think it's sexy.

Daddy: I can't imagine a thing about you I won't find absolutely perfect.

He seems so sure. I lean against the counter, staring at my phone while I try to make a decision.

Daddy: I don't want to pressure you, or rush things, but I can't stop dreaming of holding you. I want you in my arms, in my bed, filling up all the drab corners of my life. Come to the party.

BraveBoy: Okay, I'll come.

A rush of nerves and excitement washes over me. I just agreed to meet Daddy. In just a few days I'll know what he looks like, what kind of cologne he wears…or maybe he's more of a clean, natural scent type of man. Either way, I'll know soon.

> **Daddy:** Oh, my brave boy, you just made my whole day. My whole WEEK.
>
> **BraveBoy:** I'm excited. What should I wear? And I guess I need the rest of the details…
>
> **Daddy:** Leave it all to me. I'll send something over, and I'll have a car pick you up on Saturday at 6 pm to take you to the party.
>
> **BraveBoy:** Sounds perfect. I can't wait.
>
> **Daddy:** Neither can I.

"Someone's lookin' awfully happy," Sterling says, leaning over the counter and grinning at me. I shove my phone back into my pocket, feeling my cheeks heat, unable to keep the smile off my face.

"Daddy invited m-me to a p-p-party this Saturday."

His face lights up. "The costume party?"

"He said m-m-mm-masquerade."

Sterling waves his hand dismissively. "That's just a fancy word for costume party."

"D-does that mean you're going?" I'm not

sure if the thought of meeting the man I've been chatting with for months is more or less intimidating with my friends there. Oh god, does that mean Kiernan will be there too?

"Everybody's goin'. I got this real fancy peacock mask and a teal suit I'm gonna wear."

"S-s-sss-sounds awesome."

"It's gonna be. I'm so excited you're comin'. Why don't you come over, and we can get ready together?"

I give a sharp shake of my head. "Daddy s-said he'd send a car for me to my place."

"Okay, we'll come to you then. Nolan isn't in charge of this event for a change, so we were gonna get ready together anyway. We can all come to your place."

"Okay." I grin again, getting more excited about the idea by the second.

I spend the rest of the day with a huge smile on my lips, daydreaming a million different scenarios for Saturday. Something tells me I'm going to be up late writing each and every one into a new short story. Good thing Kiernan insisted I take a nap.

As I jog up the steps to my apartment several hours later, I find another present waiting for me. My cock perks up immediately, remembering the last two gifts Daddy sent. This box is significantly larger than the other two, so I'm not sure if I should be nervous or excited about what could be inside.

I pick it up and step inside, kicking off my shoes and carrying the box into my kitchen so I can set it down and open it up. An excited squeal escapes me when I reach inside to find a basket full of bath products from glittery unicorn bombs to vanilla-scented bubble bath. There are candles, loofahs, and even an inflatable pillow to attach to the tub as a head rest. I am in bath heaven. A folded piece of paper catches my attention.

Brave Boy,

I've been imagining pampering you in my large tub, but then I thought, why wait? Relax and enjoy yourself.

Until Saturday

XOXO,

Daddy

I grin, holding the piece of paper close to my chest. I hope the man is ready for the blowjob of a lifetime when we meet because he seriously has it coming.

I put all of the items back into the basket and carry it to my bathroom. I start the water and get everything set up—lighting the candles, adding some of the goodies to the water, attaching the pillow to the side of the tub—and then I snap a picture to send to Daddy with a thank you message.

I groan happily when I slip into the warm, bubbly water.

If this is what having a Daddy is like, I can't believe I waited this long. I just hope he's as amazing in person…and that he kisses as good as I've been imagining.

I'll know in a few days.

CHAPTER 13

Emerson

My door buzzes, and I hurry to let my friends in. My stomach has been dancing with a combination of impatience and terror all morning long, and now I'm sure that at least half my nausea is because I haven't had a thing to eat all day.

Sterling, Nolan, and Gannon all file into my apartment carrying garment bags. Nolan has another bag as well—I'm assuming for makeup.

"S-s-ss-sorry my place is s-small," I apologize as they start to take over the living room with their things.

"It's perfect," Nolan assures me, unzipping his suit bag to reveal a pristine white suit.

As promised, Daddy sent over a box last night, but I haven't opened it yet. While the rest of them pull out their suits, I ease the lid off the large box to find a black eye mask with delicate beading, along with a solid black three-piece suit and black button-up shirt. There's a note in the box that I pull out to read.

> *Brave Boy,*
>
> *I couldn't find you a Batman costume. I hope this will do.*
>
> *XOXO,*
>
> *Daddy*

I grin, folding the note up carefully. The other three are undressing shamelessly right here in the living room, so I follow suit, stripping out of my clothes and putting on the suit. It fits like a dream, and the fabric is impossibly soft against my skin.

"That is gorgeous," Nolan comments, reaching over to feel the fabric and practically purring. "It's *expensive*."

Heat rises in my cheeks, and I shrug. It's a nice suit, that's true, but all I really care about tonight is finally meeting Daddy in person. I could go naked or in a million-dollar suit; it wouldn't make a difference either way as long as Daddy likes me, as long as he wants to keep me.

All three of them look incredible in their suits as well. Sterling's is a striking teal, just like he said it would be, and Gannon is dressed all in red. He has the top few buttons of his dress shirt undone, exposing the rough patch of scaring that extends along the side of his neck and down to his chest.

"Don't I have a handsome date?" Nolan preens when he sees me looking at Gannon.

Gannon grunts. "Not a date."

"Oh, hush, you know what I mean."

Nolan's mask is white, just like his suit, and he attaches a halo to the top of his head as well, contrasting with the red, horned mask Gannon puts on.

I slip my own mask into place, and Nolan studies me. "You know what you need?"

"W-w-what?" I ask.

Without answering, he opens his other bag and starts rifling through it. After a few seconds, he pulls out a tube of lipstick, uncapping it and showing me the deep red color. "You have a gorgeous mouth; this will make it pop. Your man won't be able to resist you."

I'm not sure about all that, but I take the lipstick anyway. It certainly can't hurt. It's a costume party after all.

"So who do you think he is?" Sterling asks conversationally while Nolan applies some more makeup of his own, and Sterling messes around with his hair in front of my hallway mirror.

"Who?" I ask.

"Your Daddy. Do you think you know him? Or is he a total mystery?"

More nervous excitement dances through my stomach, and I think back to that first night we started talking. I thought it might be Kiernan, but he already has another M4M profile. That hasn't stopped a small part of me from wondering for the past few months though. Some people have two profiles, don't they? And his voice sounds so familiar…

I don't want to get stuck on one idea though. If he's *not* Kiernan, he's still Daddy.

"I d-don't know."

"How exciting," Nolan says, his own lips a gorgeous ruby color now, his cheeks sparkling with glitter. In spite of Gannon's statement about it not being a date, he can't seem to stop looking at the man.

The alarm on my phone pings, letting me know it's six o'clock and my car should be downstairs, so we all head down together.

An excited sound escapes me when I realize it's not just a *car*; Daddy sent a limo.

"Looks like you've found a good one." Nolan waggles his eyebrows, and we all pile in.

I fidget in my seat, tugging on my lapels and crossing and uncrossing my legs during the excruciatingly long and yet somehow impossibly short drive to the venue.

"It's gonna be great," Sterling assures me, putting a hand on my knee. "He'll love you."

My heart is hammering so hard against my ribcage I'm surprised it doesn't crack something, and my hands are starting to sweat. "I'm n-n-n-nn..." I huff in frustration when the word gets hopelessly stuck. "I w-w-w-wwww..." I shoot Sterling a helpless look as if to say *see, I can't even manage to get a sentence out right now*.

"If you're too nervous to talk, use your mouth for somethin' else," he suggests with a wicked grin, startling a laugh out of me.

He's right though. I already know Daddy. We've texted for hours on end. I know him better than I've known anyone in my life, and he knows me. We don't need to talk; we need to *meet*.

I nod and take a deep breath. Everything is going to be fine.

My phone vibrates, and I reach into my pocket to check it. There's a message from Daddy waiting for me.

Daddy: I'll be waiting just inside the entrance in a navy suit and a black mask. I'm holding a rose, so you won't miss me.

BraveBoy: Okay, we're pulling up to the door now. I'll see you in a minute.

The limo slows to a stop, and I drag in several more deep breaths, holding them in my lungs and hoping like hell they'll calm me.

It's now or never.

Kiernan

I can't think of a single time in my life that I've ever been this nervous. In college, I went through an extreme sports phase: I jumped out of a helicopter and then skied down a mountain. Well, that was the plan anyway. I botched the landing and ended up in the hospital for over a month with a dozen broken bones and a severe concussion. That moment right before I jumped to my near death was far less intimidating than watching the door for Emerson's arrival.

What if he's disappointed when he realizes that *I'm* the man he's been talking to? What if he's pissed that I didn't tell him? I double check that my tie is straight and my hair is tamed, keeping my eyes fixed on the door while I fidget.

"It's going to be fine," Barrett assures me, putting his hand on my shoulder and giving it a squeeze. I didn't tell him the whole truth, instead letting him in on the fact that I invited the boy I've been speaking to from the app. Soon, everything will be out in the open, and Emerson and I will be able to move forward, building a relationship together. At least that's what I hope.

"Mm," I grunt in response. He doesn't know it will be fine, but I appreciate his optimism.

"He's right," Alden agrees, standing on my other side. "It's going to be—"

I don't have the chance to find out what he thinks it's going to be because at that moment, Gannon and Nolan walk through the door, arm in arm, dressed like a matching set—an angel and a devil—and Alden's words falter.

I don't have time to give any thought to his reaction to the two men because Emerson is right behind them, dressed in the suit and mask I sent over. I half expected to see the unicorn T-shirt underneath the suit jacket, but he put on the dress shirt that I sent as well.

He casts his eyes around for a moment,

sweeping them over me before continuing his search. My heart flails wildly, and my hand tightens reflexively around the rose I'm holding. I startle when one of the thorns bites into my palm, forcing me to loosen my grip.

Emerson frowns and then returns his attention to me. Barrett has pulled his boy away and Alden seems to have slipped away as well, leaving me standing alone, trying my best to appear more confident than I feel.

He drags his gaze over me, this time slowly enough that it lands on the rose. His breathtakingly red lips part in silent shock, his eyes snapping to mine. It's time.

I square my shoulders and take a step forward, holding the rose out toward him. "Hey there, Brave Boy. I'm glad you made it."

His chest hitches with a heavy breath, and he continues to stare at me. While a masquerade seemed like a brilliant idea at the time, I'm wishing now I could see his expression fully. Is he angry? Disappointed? Or simply stunned?

"Emerson, I—" I'm about to apologize and suggest we go somewhere to talk, but before I can get the words out, he's closing the space between us and launching himself into my arms.

My heart explodes into a gallop, and I manage to catch him without stumbling.

"Daddy," he whispers, a smile spreading over his cherry red lips. The word sends a bolt of heat through me, everything in the universe seeming to align for this unbearably perfect moment. Our mouths are drawn together like magnets, his lips parting as soon as we connect. It's slow at first, a gentle introduction that we've both been waiting entirely too long for. He yields control easily, just as perfect in person as he's been in all of our chats and calls, so sweetly submissive and eager to please.

Emerson playfully flicks his tongue against my bottom lip, and my body heats from head to toe. I growl against his mouth and kiss him deeper, harder, hungrier.

I'm sure people are staring, but I couldn't give less of a fuck. The weight of my boy in my arms is perfect. His lips are soft and sweet against mine, just a little sticky from the lipstick he has on, his tongue hot and wet as he slides it into my mouth. I let him have his fun for a minute before taking control of the kiss, sucking and nibbling and savoring his mouth. His body trembles against me, his fingers curling around the lapels of my suit jacket.

Lust and joy and a hundred other emotions rush through me all at once. Nothing in my life has ever felt this right. Emerson is *mine,* and I'm never going to let him go.

I break the kiss so we can both get our bearings and perhaps take this somewhere a little more private. The crimson lipstick Emerson has on is smeared around his mouth now, no doubt painting mine as well, which is a thought I'm rather fond of. He looked incredible when he stepped through the door, nicely dressed and ready for a fancy evening. But he looks even better now, slightly debauched by me.

"It's y-y-y-you." He tightens his grip on my suit jacket, and I nod.

"It's me," I confirm with a wry smirk. He loosens his legs from around my waist and slides down my body so he's standing on his own again. "Why don't I grab us a couple of drinks, and we can go somewhere to talk?"

Emerson tugs his bottom lip between his teeth and looks up at me through his eyelashes, exactly how I've been imagining for weeks… months even. "C-c-can we talk l-l-l-lll…" He pauses and licks his lips. "After?" he finishes.

"After?" I repeat, following his gaze as he looks at the mass of masked guests dancing a few feet away while trays of food and drinks are carried by waiters dressed in white tuxedos. "Of course. I'm an idiot. I invited you to a party just to immediately try to drag you away for a boring conversation."

He gives me a crooked smile and shrugs. He's absolutely right; we should enjoy the party and each other. Now that I know he's not about to run away screaming from me, there will be plenty of time to discuss things later...and hopefully plenty more of those addictive kisses.

I wrap my hand around his, slotting our fingers together neatly. His smaller hand fits so perfectly in mine, just like his petite body fit in my arms. Jesus, I need to keep a handle on myself, or I'll end up scaring the poor boy off.

I smile and nod at several people as we make our way onto the dance floor, greeting acquaintances and shrugging off curious looks at my date for the evening. It's rare that I show up to an event with someone unrecognizable, typically sticking with the same gold-digging twinks who worm their way into every society party.

When I find a good spot, I pull Emerson close, keeping our hands clasped while I guide the other to my shoulder and wrap my free arm around his waist. A worried expression tightens his features, and he gestures for me to lean down so he can whisper something to me.

"I d-d-don't know how to d-d-dance like this."

I tighten my arm around his waist and turn my head to press a soft kiss to his cheek. "All you have to do is follow my lead. I think you can handle that, right, sweetheart?"

He bobs his head in a quick nod. "Yes, Daddy," he answers softly, and my heart nearly explodes out of my chest. That word on his lips is even more perfect than I'd imagined. Even hearing it the second time, it's effect on me hasn't dulled. Will it nearly bring me to my knees every time this sweet, beautiful boy calls me his Daddy? I suppose that's a fair enough price to pay. I'll just have to dedicate the rest of my life to ensuring I earn such a privilege from him.

I waltz us around the dance floor, keeping my boy nice and close, occasionally leaning in to whisper scandalous gossip into his ear about people I spot. Emerson gasps and laughs each time, always holding onto me tighter like he's afraid I'm going to slip away at any moment.

Barrett catches my eye, giving me a curious expression when he sees that it's Emerson I'm dancing with. He'll no doubt be pestering me to hear the whole story later. Based on the look Sterling is giving Emerson, I won't be the only one fielding questions from friends. But that's a problem for another day. Tonight is about enjoying my first date with my boy.

"How about a drink?" I suggest after a few dances, and he nods, releasing his grip on my shoulder and letting me lead him off the dance floor.

I snag two glasses of wine from the first waiter I spot, offering one to Emerson. I find us a table, pulling out a chair for him and then taking the seat beside him. He seems to be enthralled with the house...mansion really, his eyes wide as he looks around at the high ceilings and grand staircase that frames the dance floor.

Is this the kind of place Emerson dreams of living? Does he fantasize about a man who will buy him expensive things and drape him in all the finest clothes? I bristle a little internally, not truly thinking of him, but of all the boys before who always seemed to become extra affectionate toward me after I would shower them in gifts or take them on luxurious vacations. I wasn't a Daddy in their eyes; I was a wallet.

"Something wrong?" Emerson asks quietly, putting a hand on top of mine and looking at me with big, soft eyes.

I flip my hand over and clasp his. "No, Brave Boy," I assure him, lifting his hand to my lips and kissing the back of it.

He blushes, his eyes locked on mine the whole time. "I c-c-c-can't believe this is r-r-real. I h-h-hoped..."

My heart leaps again. He hoped for me? Is that what he means? Fuck, I was afraid to wish for that much, to hope he might be imagining me on the other end of the phone just like I was imagining him.

"The night we first started talking, I hoped it was you too," I confess. "I knew before tonight..." I want to be completely honest with him. If we're going to go headfirst into this relationship, I don't want any secrets hanging between us.

He squeezes my hand. "A f-few more dances and th-then we can l-leave and talk?"

"Anything you want," I agree, kissing his hand again and taking a sip from my wine. There's no rush. I'm simply eager to have everything completely out in the open between us. But he's right. I would rather take him home for that discussion. I wonder if he'll be open to spending the night in my bed. I ache with longing at the thought of spending the night with my boy wrapped in my arms.

I turn the conversation toward more insignificant topics while we both sip our drinks. I snag some appetizers from waiters who pass and, before long, Em seems to be relaxing, stuttering less and smiling while we discuss the book he sent me home with the other day.

We do end up dancing again, waltzing to the live music until our feet are sore. The best part of the evening is the way my boy laughs so beautifully when I spin him on the dance floor. He relaxes when I dip him, trusting his weight to my strong arm around his back. The subtle show of submission, of putting his faith in the knowledge that I wouldn't let harm come to him, is enough to make my dick hard and my heart soft all at once.

I pull him upright and duck my head to whisper into his ear.

"How would you like to come back to my place and enjoy the pool with me?"

Emerson leans into me, his earlobe brushing against my lips and his fingers tightening against my shoulder. "I don't have a s-swimsuit."

"Even better," I purr, and he makes a small noise that I almost don't hear over the din of the party. It's a sweet, needy noise that makes my already hard cock throb.

Tonight isn't a night for sex though. Tonight, we're going to talk, swim, and hopefully fall asleep together. After everything is on the table, and Emerson has had the chance to sleep on things, we can go from there.

"L-let's go."

CHAPTER 14

Emerson

I feel like I'm in a living daydream. It's Kiernan. After all of the wishing and hoping, Lonely-Daddy is Kiernan. I wave to Sterling as we pass him on our way out to Kiernan's car. He mouths *call me,* and I nod in agreement. I'll call him, but not tonight. Tonight, Daddy and I have a lot to talk about, but I hope that's not the only thing that will keep us busy.

My cock starts to harden as I imagine all the things he might want to do to me, all the ways he'll worship and use my body. A quiet whine slips out of my lips, and he casts a curious look at me over his shoulder, pausing for his driver to open the car door for us. I lick my lips and stare up at him, eagerly picturing the two of us naked, his massive body all mine to climb and rub against.

He quirks an eyebrow at me, a wicked grin spreading over his lips as if he can read my mind. "Behave," he says, and a shiver of desire ripples through me. When I realized it was him earlier,

I had a brief moment of wondering *how* I didn't recognize his voice on the phone. It's because his Daddy voice is different: deeper, somehow both commanding and softer at the same time, like the sound equivalent of a simultaneous warm hug and a slap on the ass.

"Yes, Daddy," I answer without giving it a second thought, and his gaze heats.

The driver steps away, climbing into the front seat of the car while Kiernan gestures for me to get in. I slip past him and slide all the way in, the buttery leather of the seats like a dream. Oh god, he'll be horrified if he ever rides in my car. My passenger seat has a large duct tape patch over the torn worn-out upholstery. Not that I couldn't buy a newer car if I wanted; it's just nowhere near the top of my list of things to worry about.

Kiernan gets in behind me. "Buckle up," he says firmly, and I hurry to obey. Will he call me a good boy like he did on the phone? Fuck, I want to hear those words on his lips while he pins me down, naked and horny beneath him.

My cock twitches and another quiet sound tries to force its way out of my throat, but I manage to swallow it back. I'm going to behave, just like he said. For now, at least.

The car starts to move, and I slide my hand onto the middle seat between us, hoping he'll reach for it. Kiernan doesn't disappoint, twining our fingers together, his large hand practically swallowing mine up.

Now that we're away from all the noise of the party, and the initial shock of discovering the truth about Daddy, my mind starts to buzz with thoughts and questions. What does all of this mean? Does Kiernan feel the same way I do? Daddy promised me so many things about what would happen once we met, but I'm having a hard time reconciling the two men in my mind into one. As much time as I spent hoping they were one and the same, Daddy still *feels* like someone else.

But there's one question pushing its way to the forefront of my mind, and I think I'm ready to ask now.

"When d-d-did you know?" I ask, keeping my gaze focused outside the window, watching as the lights of the neighborhood fade and we head in a toward less populated area. I remember him saying his house was somewhere dark and quiet, where we'd be able to see the stars.

"I had my suspicions early on, and the unicorn safeword was a bit of a flashing sign," he says, and I giggle. "But I knew for sure after the night we had dinner. You went home and texted me about your guilt, and I knew."

I think back over all of our interactions.

Did he change when he realized who I was? Not that I can remember. But he *did* encourage me to give Kiernan a chance...give *him* a chance? This is kind of confusing. I finally tear my eyes away from the window and look over at him. Can I trust him?

My grandpa always used to tell me that I was too naïve, that I let people manipulate me because I was so desperate to be liked. I know he was right, but what I don't know is if that's what's happening right now.

Was LonelyDaddy some elaborate scheme for Kiernan to trick me and seduce me? It's almost laughable to consider. Why would anyone go to that much trouble to get *me* into bed? I can't shake the uneasy feeling all the same.

He's completely quiet, not offering any defense or explanation, simply holding my hand and waiting for me to sort through the confusing tangle of thoughts I'm wrestling with.

Before I manage to get my head straight, we pull into his driveway.

He helps me out of the car, and I look up at the looming house. It's exactly what I've pictured any time I let my mind wander down the path of Kiernan bringing me home. Of course, in all of my fantasies, we can't keep our hands off of each other as we stumble inside, our mouths fused while we grope to strip each other bare.

Not that I'm ruling all of that out, once I'm sure I can trust him.

Kiernan dismisses his driver and leads me up the stone steps to his front door. I notice a tenseness to his shoulders when he stops to unlock the door. Maybe he's as nervous and confused as I am. Maybe we're both a bit out of our element right now.

"Are you hungry? Thirsty?" he offers as soon as we're inside.

"I could eat s-s-s-sss-something small," I answer.

"Why don't I show you to the pool, and then you can relax and enjoy the view while I put a snack tray together for us."

"Okay."

I follow him through the house, stopping at the back door to take off my shoes and then walking out onto the patio. It's absolutely beautiful, an infinity pool that looks like you could swim right off the edge, a seating area with a couch and chairs as well as a separate row of loungers. On the far end of the patio, I spot what looks like a sauna as well as a hot tub. His house is like a five-star resort.

"Make yourself comfortable, and I'll be back in a few minutes," he says before disappearing back inside the house.

I loosen the top few buttons on my dress shirt, sauntering over and sitting down on one of the lounge chairs next to the pool.

Make myself comfortable...does that mean I should get naked? It *was* implied before we left the party, but that was before I let my thoughts complicate everything. My hands start to sweat, my heart beating faster with the uncomfortable feeling of uncertainty.

I swallow around the tight feeling in my throat and try again to work through my jumbled emotions. Am I upset that Kiernan has known the truth for weeks and let me go on thinking I didn't know him?

I try to imagine what I would have done if I'd known. It was early enough that I might've clammed up, gotten nervous wondering what Kiernan might be thinking of me, where things were going, if I was saying and doing the right things. It was easy with LonelyDaddy because he didn't put any pressure or expectations on me. I've wanted Kiernan so badly since the minute we met that I'm not sure if I would've had the confidence to get to know him the way I did when I thought he was someone else. LonelyDaddy made me brave.

I pull my phone out of my pocket and scroll to the conversation when I told him about dinner with Kiernan so I can remind myself of exactly what he said at the time. The gap in time between my confession and his response is like a snapshot of his hesitation. He got confirmation of my identity, and he took a few minutes to gather his thoughts before responding.

It's obvious he wasn't lying about discovering the truth at that moment. Then he tried to nudge me to stop messaging him and instead get to know Kiernan in person. I told him no. I said I wasn't ready and that our chats were what I needed. The knot in my chest loosens as I read back over that conversation.

I told Daddy what I needed, and he gave it to me.

Since the very first message he sent, he's been patient and sweet. He's been everything I was afraid to even hope for in a man. I glance back toward the house, my heart stuttering now with a different kind of nerves. This thing between us could be so good; all I have to do is be brave enough to jump and know he'll catch me.

With new resolve, I finish undoing the buttons on my shirt, shrugging off my jacket and shirt and laying both on the chair.

Kiernan

I take my time cutting up various fruits

and arranging them neatly on the tray. I want to give Emerson the chance to gather his thoughts before I go out there and plead my case, explain to him my reasoning for keeping him in the dark and hope like hell he'll understand.

I could practically see the moment in the car that the reality of the situation crashed down around him. I had a feeling it might once the party was behind us.

I add some crackers and a few different types of cheese to the tray as well, and then grab a couple of water bottles from the refrigerator. Balancing everything in one hand, I tug open the glass door and step outside. My eyes do a quick sweep of the patio, finally landing on Emerson lounging next to the pool, laid out on a nautical chaise, his eyes closed like he's sunbathing. I take in the peaceful expression on his face for a few moments, a sense of tranquility settling over me as well. Maybe I haven't botched things too terribly.

I drag my eyes off of his face, and my breath catches. The boy is completely nude. I was careful to leave my invitation for him to get comfortable open-ended, not wanting him to think I had any specific expectations for what that would look like. But maybe that caused him to get nervous and attempt to guess what I might want.

Setting the snack tray down on the glass table next to the outdoor couch, I stride over to Emerson, making my steps loud so I won't startle him with too quiet of an approach. As I near him, his eyes open slowly, a smile tilting the corner of his lips.

"I hope you know that nudity wasn't a condition of being here," I say delicately, forcing my eyes to remain on his face until I'm sure we're clear on the subject. He may have sent me dozens of beautifully pornographic images over the past few weeks, pictures of nearly every inch of his petite, tempting body, but this is an entirely different situation.

"You said to g-g-get comfortable," he points out, sitting up and swinging his legs over the side of the chair to face me. In his seated position, he has to crane his neck to look up at me, the long line of his neck beyond tempting. I wonder how he would feel about a collar…when the time is right, of course.

"And you're comfortable like this for our conversation?" I check, and he nods, not making any move to cover himself up.

I finally give in and let my gaze roam over him. He's even more stunning bathed in moonlight than in the pictures he sent. He's not skin and bones, nor is he waxed to the point of hairlessness like most boys I've dated. He's all lean muscles and a dusting of dark hair, his cock half hard, resting against his thigh. I offer him my hand, and he takes it, letting me pull him to his feet.

While I lead him over to the patio couch, I slow my steps momentarily so I can catch a quick glimpse at his backside, grinning to myself when I catch sight of the tattoo on his right butt cheek. If we make it past this conversation tonight, I'll have to ask why he lied about it.

Emerson picks a fat, ripe strawberry off the tray and takes a seat on the couch while I shrug out of my suit jacket and kick off my shoes, otherwise remaining fully clothed. I love the feeling of staying dressed while my boy is bare for me, fully on display and eager to be touched.

Not that we'll be touching tonight, I remind myself. There are too many important things to discuss, not the least of which being the dynamics of a potential relationship. We talked about these things as LonelyDaddy and BraveBoy, but now we need to agree to them as Emerson and Kiernan.

"I want to start by saying that I'm sorry for not being honest with you. I need you to know that I struggled with what would be best for you, and the choice I made was purely based on your needs."

"I know," he says easily before wrapping

his lips around the strawberry in the most obscene way possible, his eyes fixed on mine the entire time. My cock swells, caressed by the soft material of my boxer briefs. He chews slowly and then drags his tongue over his bottom lip, gathering the lingering juices from the fruit. In the moonlight it's hard to tell if there are any remnants of lipstick left on his mouth or if it was all kissed away. "S-s-sit down?" He pats the cushion next to him when he finishes chewing.

I didn't realize I was still towering over him until he said something. I take the spot he indicated, making myself comfortable. As soon as I'm seated, Emerson eyes my lap shyly, nibbling that plump bottom lip of his.

"If you'd be more comfortable having this conversation over here, then by all means." I gesture to my lap. That's all the invitation he seems to need, scrambling over and making himself comfortable, his head against my shoulder and his butt squarely against my rapidly hardening cock.

He leans forward and grabs a few more pieces of fruit off the tray, shifting his weight against me and rubbing his perky ass over my cock. I should get some sort of medal for managing to stay focused. But this conversation is important.

"We discussed a lot of things online," I say,

and Em nods. It's too dark to tell, but the bashful way he ducks his head makes me think he's blushing again. Such a sweet blush he has. I'm eager for the chance to lay him down in proper light and chase the flush of his skin with my lips. I want to worship every single inch of his body and tell him what a good, perfect boy he is until he's overflowing with my praise and there isn't a doubt in his mind that he's already mine.

"I still m-m-mm-mean it all."

My heart swells and triples its beats. "You want to be my boy? Even though I withheld information from you?" I ask. "You trust me to be your Daddy?"

He nods his head rapidly. "I n-needed it."

I wrap my arms around him and hold him a little tighter. Is this real? It's hard not to get my hopes up that Emerson might be the boy I've been dreaming of for years now, the boy I can share my home and my life with.

"I'll always put your needs before everything else," I promise him. He leans into me, putting one hand against my chest and bunching the front of my dress shirt with the other. A soft sigh falls from his lips and ghosts over my neck.

"I know."

Those two simple words are everything I was almost afraid to hope for. Every inch of his trust is contained within that simple statement, and it's worth more than every dollar in my vast bank account.

I turn my head and press a soft kiss to his forehead. He leans into my touch, tightening his grip on the front of my shirt and wiggling his ass against my erection again.

"Can w-w-we have sex n-n-now?" he asks, sounding the slightest bit breathless, an almost irresistible edge of neediness in his voice.

I chuckle, my lips still against his forehead. "Not so fast, sweetheart." I pull back and card my fingers through his hair. "I'm glad you understand why I didn't tell you the truth sooner, but I still think you should take a night to sleep on things, to let them settle."

Emerson frowns. "I d-don't need to," he says stubbornly before purposefully grinding his ass against my erection again, with a pointed look like he thinks he's winning this round.

I slide my hand down to his thigh, holding him in place and thrusting my hard, throbbing cock against him. His smug smile widens. Silly boy. I lean in, brushing my nose against his earlobe and then giving it a playful nip. Emerson shivers, his own cock hardening between his legs, thickening, and starting to stand up.

"Daddy said no," I whisper near his ear, and

his breath catches and then turns into a frustrated whine. "Here are your options: we can take a swim, finish our snack, and then crawl into my big, soft bed and fall asleep together."

"Or?" he asks, eyeing the pool. He doesn't seem opposed to option one; he just wants to see what's behind door number two before he commits. Smart boy.

"Or you can get dressed and I'll drive you home. Then I can come pick you up in the morning and take you to breakfast so we can talk more."

"The first one," he answers quickly.

"I was hoping that's the one you would pick," I confess, lifting him off my lap and setting him back down beside me.

He starts to protest until he realizes I'm unbuttoning my shirt.

"C-can I help?" Emerson asks eagerly.

Jesus, he's sweet. I stop working the buttons open and stand up, turning to face him. "Go ahead and undress me," I offer, letting my arms hang at my sides as he quickly gets up on his knees and picks up where I left off, undoing one button at a time until my shirt is hanging open. He lets out a quiet whimper, staring in awe at my chest covered in a blanket of auburn hair. I've been slacking on my gym time for the past year or so, my once firm muscles now covered by a soft layer.

It's clear Emerson isn't disappointed by my lack of a six-pack, hurriedly pushing my shirt off and then running his greedy hands along my belly and up to my chest, his eyes devouring my body before returning to my face.

"So sexy, Daddy," he murmurs, leaning forward and brushing a kiss against the center of my chest, sending a rush of heat and affection all the way down to my toes.

"Finish with my clothes, Brave Boy, so we can go for a swim."

He nods and gets back to work, undoing my belt and then opening my pants. My erection strains against my underwear, and my boy licks his lips, reaching for it.

"Emerson." I say his name sternly, and he pulls his hand back and looks up at me with a full-on pout.

"I c-c-c-c-c…"

"I said not tonight," I remind him when he stops struggling with what he wants to say and licks his lips. His expression tightens, his pout turning more genuine, no longer appearing to be just for show. "What's wrong?"

He gives a sharp shake of his head, hooking his fingers in the waistband of my underwear and yanking them down. My cock springs free, thick and heavy with arousal. It sways between my legs, my balls just as weighty, aching for a relief that isn't going to come tonight.

I step out of my pants and underwear once they're around my ankles and then offer a hand to Emerson to help him up. He puts his hand in mine, letting me guide him over to the pool.

"You do know how to swim, don't you?" I check, stopping just short of the pool steps.

He rolls his eyes. These are the types of things it's easy to miss over texting. I had him pegged as an all-around sweet, pliant boy, and he is, but there's also the barest hint of a brat just waiting to feel secure enough to be unleashed. "Yes, Daddy," he answers, sounding rather put out.

"Too bad. You would've looked cute in the orange life vest I have stashed around here somewhere," I tease, and he giggles.

I step into the lukewarm water. Even with the heat outside, I prefer my pool be kept around eighty-five degrees. Emerson wades in behind me, making a pleased noise as the water surrounds him. Once we're waist deep, he lets go of my hand and dives into the water, his body slicing through the calm surface as he swims to the far end of the pool and then flips around and swims back, clearly showing off.

"Swim team?" I guess when he pops up in front of me again, splashing water in all directions.

"All through h-high school," he answers with a grin. "Would you really have m-m-made me wear a l-life jacket?"

"If you needed one," I reply simply, although I suspect we would've stayed in the shallow end if he couldn't swim.

He smiles, a sweet, hopeful kind of smile that warms me from the inside. But then a thought seems to occur to him. He tilts his head and wades a few feet in front of me.

"Do you l-l-like a boy who y-you can baby?"

"Age play?" I ask, and he nods. "To be honest, it's not my particular kink. But I'm going to tip my hand here and tell you that I like you quite a bit, and if it's something you need, I'd be willing to give it a try."

"No," he answers. "I w-w-was going to s-s-ss-say the same."

I swim a little closer, and he playfully floats farther away with a teasing grin.

"Okay, so we'll both be adults," I conclude.

"*N-naked* adults," he points out, looking down at our bare bodies, illuminated by the pool lights and distorted by the water.

"Such a horny boy," I tsk, reaching out and snagging him by the wrist. It's easy to tug him close in the water, his body floating toward me while he laughs and then crashes into me. I wrap one arm around him and use my free hand to brush his wet hair off of his forehead.

"Is that okay?" he asks, his voice dripping with insecurity.

"More than okay," I assure him, ducking my head for a kiss.

I can taste the saltwater on his lips, contrasting the sweetness of the fruit he was munching on. He wraps his legs around my hips and his arms around my neck, trusting his full weight to me and parting his lips so I can ravage his mouth. His hard cock presses against my belly, my own bumping the curve of his ass while I coax his tongue to play with mine.

"Daddy," he whimpers, nearly trembling in my arms, squirming to hump his erection against me.

"Shh." I try to settle him, slowing the kisses to something sweeter, continuing to slide my tongue and my lips against his. My attempt at soothing seems to have the opposite effect, my boy tensing a bit, some of his pliancy vanishing. I break the kiss and look at him. "What's wrong?" I ask for the second time, prepared to push it if I have to in order to find out what's bothering him.

Emerson starts to shake his head again but stops when he notices my stern expression. "Do you n-n-not w-w-w-w..." He pauses and licks his lips. "W-w-w-why w-w-w-w-..." He huffs in frustration, clearly getting himself too worked up and tongue-tied to get out what he's trying to say.

"Why won't I fuck you tonight?" I guess, and he gives a sharp nod. "I already told you why. I want you to have a night to sleep on things, to be sure of your feelings before we jump into anything physical."

"W-w-we've had sex," he says.

In spite of the irritation and insecurity etched on his features, his statement brings a smile to my lips—still tingling from our kiss. I've been with too many men who only consider it sex if there's penetration, relegating everything else to lesser. The fact that Emerson views the intimacy we've already shared as equally valuable as in-person sex speaks volumes. It's not about where someone sticks their dick or even about getting each other off. Sex is about choosing to share the deepest possible level of intimacy with someone, and I think Emerson might be the first man I've been with who understands that.

"Then humor me," I suggest. "I want to spend the night drunk on just your lips, imagining the pleasure we'll find in each other's bodies later. A little delayed gratification never hurt anyone, has it?"

"Debatable," he groans, thrusting against me again. "But you *do* w-w-want me?"

"Oh, my Brave Boy, I want you more than I want my next breath."

He smiles and then offers me his sweetly parted lips again, his eyelids fluttering closed before my mouth even meets his.

We swim and kiss until our hands are pruned and both of our stomachs are growling, and then we get out of the pool and dry off. We lie down on the patio couch, Emerson tucked close with one leg hitched over mine, his head resting in the crook of my arm, and feed each other bites of fruit and cheese until the tray is nothing but crumbs.

While we eat, we talk again about books and some of Emerson's favorite plays.

"I w-w-wanted to try out for *West S-s-ss-side Story* so bad in high school," he confesses, licking the last bit of watermelon juice off of his fingers.

"Why didn't you?" I ask, and he fixes me with a look that screams *be serious*. "I would've been in the audience every night." I kiss the top of his head.

"You're too n-n-nice; you'll ruin m-me," he

warns.

"Good, then I'll have to keep you all for myself."

The look Emerson gives me is full of disbelief and hope. He's not sure yet that I really want to keep him. That's okay; I have all the time in the world to prove it to him.

Eventually, he starts to yawn. I usher him inside, leaving him alone for a few minutes to get ready for bed. I tidy up my bedroom a little and straighten out my sheets, climbing under them and resting my back against the headboard to wait for him.

When he comes out of the bathroom, there's a shyness about him again that's absolutely endearing. He almost tiptoes to the empty side of the bed and then lingers there, waiting for my permission to get in.

"Come here, sexy boy." I pull back the sheet and crook a finger at him. He grins and climbs in, scooting close to me. "I thought I'd read a chapter for you. Do you remember where we left off last time?" I check, picking my book up off the nightstand while Emerson rests his head against my thigh. He nods while I card my fingers through his drying hair, clearing my throat and picking up at the chapter where I left off when I read to him the other night on the phone.

It only takes a few pages before he's snoring softly. I tuck my bookmark back between the pages and carefully sink down to lay my head on the pillow, moving his head up to my chest. He murmurs something sleepily, wrapping his arms around me as if he's afraid I'm going to get away.

Silly boy. As if I'd go anywhere when my bed finally has my boy in it.

CHAPTER 15

Emerson

The unfamiliar surroundings when I open my eyes should be disorienting, but even still half-asleep, I remember every second of last night. Kiernan's arms around me, his lips on mine in the pool, the tender way he fed me fruit and cheese while we lay on the patio couch, the deep, soothing voice reading me to sleep. It was the most incredible night of my entire night.

He's still fast asleep while I slowly wake up. I'm not sure if he did it consciously or we simply ended up this way during the night, but his body is spooned around me, holding me close. The vast expanse of his bare skin is hot against mine, both of us slightly sticky with sweat. His cock is resting against my butt, half hard but fucking *massive*.

I wiggle against him and feel it thicken and stiffen. My hole flutters, and my own cock gets hard, imagining him rolling me onto my belly, pinning me down, and sinking inside me. My breath catches at the thought.

I want to feel trapped under him. I want both of my hands caught in his and held over my head so I'm at his mercy while he uses me for his pleasure. My hand twitches toward my erection, but I know I shouldn't touch…not until Daddy says so anyway. Fuck, that thought forces another quiet gasp from my lips, my cock throbbing.

Kiernan makes a rumbly noise in his sleep, the sound vibrating against my back. He tightens his arms around me, but otherwise seems to stay asleep. I take a deep breath and try to calm myself down. It's not easy. I feel like a teenager discovering my own dick for the first time. I've been with plenty of men over the years, but never anyone I could tell my fantasies to or trusted enough to explore my kinkier whims with. Until now.

It's exhilarating and centering all at once. Somehow, I feel like a live wire and yet unbelievably calm at the same time. I think it's because I know Kiernan will take care of me.

I squirm in his arms until his grasp on me loosens enough that I can roll over to face him. His face is placid with sleep, so I take the opportunity to simply stare at him. I'm still having a hard time believing I got everything I was hoping for. Not only that Kiernan was the one on the other side of the computer screen, but that he seems to be just as perfect of a Daddy in real life as he seemed to be online.

As much as I wanted to tempt him into fucking me right there in the pool last night, I'm glad he didn't. If all I am to him is a quick fuck, he could've had me already and then put me in a car and sent me home. But he didn't. He kissed me like it was the only thing he wanted to do and then fed me snacks and read me to sleep. It made me feel…cared for. Emotion tightens around my throat. It's been a long time since I felt as important to someone as Kiernan made me feel last night. Not since my grandpa died.

I run my fingers over the wiry hair of his beard, and the muscles in his face twitch. His eyelids flutter but don't quite open. He must be a very sound sleeper. I grin, a sense of mischief filling me as I wonder what I'd have to do to wake him up.

I put both hands in his beard and squish his face in my hands. He grunts in his sleep but doesn't wake up. I giggle and consider my next move. Dragging my hands down to his chest, my cock gets interested in the situation again. He's so big. Not just the fun bits between his legs, but all over. I have a giant Viking Daddy who's going to be able to throw me around if he wants to. I groan and grind against his large, hairy thigh.

Focus, I scold myself. I'm supposed to be *waking* Daddy not humping him. As fun as the latter may be.

His nipples harden when I run my hands over them, his breathing increasing and his big, thick cock jerking against my stomach. But he *still* doesn't wake up.

I loved the cuddly look of his body and all the thick red hair on his chest and belly in the pictures he sent, but it's *so* much better in person. I hope Daddy has *lots* of naked time on the agenda for us. Even if we don't have sex again yet, I want to enjoy every inch of him.

More determined than ever to wake him, I tweak his nipples, managing to get another grunt and a reaction from his cock, but he still doesn't wake up. I find a nice soft spot on his belly and attempt to tickle him, nothing. I lick his face for god's sake and still *nothing*. Huffing in frustration, I nibble on the tip of his nose, and the man sleeps right through it. He should be studied by scientists.

"Daddy," I whisper his name, expecting it to be just as fruitless as the rest of my tactics, but his eyes pop open instantly.

They're unfocused at first, full of sleepy confusion. But as soon as awareness dawns on his expression, a smile spreads over his face…followed by a bewildered frown. "Why is my cheek wet?" He reaches up and wipes it with the back of his hand.

"You wouldn't wake up, so I l-l-ll-licked you," I explain.

"Seems reasonable," he deadpans.

"I thought so." I grin and wiggle closer, burying my face against his chest and taking a deep breath to fill my lungs with the smell of him.

"How did you sleep?" he asks, holding me nice and tight, like he's just as happy to be all close and cuddly as I am.

"S-s-so good," I answer with a yawn. Now that he's awake, I feel kind of sleepy again. It's Sunday, so I don't have to go open Unicorn Books until noon. Maybe we can spend the whole morning in bed together.

"Mm, me too," he says, sounding content, his voice a little more gravelly than usual and his skin still warm from sleep. "In fact, I might have to lure you into my bed more often."

"Okay," I agree easily, finally pulling my face away from his chest and tilting my head back so I can see his face, needing to tell if he's just being a sweet talker or if he really means it.

He looks down at me with a soft, open expression that unravels something inside me. Is it too soon to fall in love with him? Probably. I should learn some serious chill before I go all eager puppy on Kiernan and scare him away.

I'm allowed to imagine it though: to think about what it might be like to let myself fall completely head over heels for this man, to share a life with him and know he'll always be there to take care of me? Maybe one day he might give me a collar like I've seen some subs wear to show that they're owned, that they're *loved*.

A whine slips out of my throat as a deep, aching need fills me.

"What, sweetheart? Tell Daddy what you need." His voice is low and commanding as his hand slips down to my ass, grabbing it with the slightest bit of roughness.

What do I need? Everything. I need his hands and his mouth all over me. I need to know I'm not the only one feeling all of these incredible and terrifying things, even if it might be a little too soon. I need to belong to him and to know he belongs to me. I can't say all of that, and not just because I'm pretty sure I'd never get it all out when I'm feeling this undone.

So, I answer in the simplest, truest way I can. "You," I whisper.

Kiernan groans, tightening his grip on the soft flesh of my ass cheek and yanking me up, putting me face to face with him so I'm not craning my neck anymore. "How do you feel this morning?"

"Horny." I grind my erection against his stomach just in case he needs proof.

He chuckles. "I meant about us, dirty boy."

Dirty boy, ungh, I like that. It's possible that I've lain awake way too many nights, thinking up sweet, filthy things I'd like to be called in the throes of passion. I wonder if I can work up the courage to ask him to call me *Daddy's Little Fuck Toy* while he fills me with his cock.

As crazy as it seems, I think Kiernan might just make me brave enough to ask him for almost anything.

"Good," I answer, rubbing my cheek against his coarse beard, loving the way it burns my skin slightly. I want him to leave beard burns and hickeys and handprints all over my body. I want to look in the mirror later and see Kiernan on every inch of my skin. "S-s-s-so good."

He kneads my ass cheeks, and I can feel the stickiness of his precum against the inside of my thigh where his cock is resting. "I know words are harder when you're nervous or excited, but I need some words here, sweetheart."

I give a whine of frustration between gritted teeth while burying my fingers in his chest hair and thrusting against him. Words are *so* stupid. "I s-s-s-slept on it. P-p-p-p-ppp...*ugh*," I groan. "Fuck me."

I don't actually care if he *fucks* me or if he'd rather get me off in a different way. Daddy's choice, as far as I'm concerned. But if he doesn't do something soon, I'm going to get myself off rubbing against him, and something tells me that's not what good boys do.

Kiernan

Emerson pants and thrusts against me shamelessly, his cock leaving streaks of precum on my stomach. I'm not doing much better, my cock achingly hard and pressed against his thigh. I woke up with his warm, petite body all wrapped around me, and I'm almost positive I've died and gone to heaven.

As much as I want to pin him down and fuck him until he screams, there are a few more things that need to be figured out first. The fact that too much talking when he's worked up seems to stress him out isn't helping matters. I want my boy to feel relaxed and taken care of, not like he has to worry about putting words together when all he wants to do is give himself over to the submission he's been waiting a lifetime to experience.

"Listen, Brave Boy, here's what we're going to do," I say, rolling him onto his back and situating myself on top of him. I'm careful not to use my full weight—I'd crush the poor boy—but just enough that he knows I'm taking over now. I use one hand to hold both of his wrists, pinning his arms above his head, and he moans, arching his body up against mine. "I don't want you to say another word, unless it's your safeword, until I tell you it's okay. Nod if you understand."

Emerson bites down on his bottom lip and nods eagerly.

"Good boy." I press a gentle kiss against his lips. "Your safeword is still unicorn, but if you don't think you can say it, for any reason, you can snap instead. Can you snap?" He snaps once to show me he can. "Perfect. That goes for any time we play."

He nods again, his cheeks flushed and his eyes fixed on me, full of open eagerness. He's writhing and squirming under me, but not making any real attempt to get his hands free from my loose restraint.

One thing I learned during all of our online chats is that Emerson may come across as shy, but he's absolutely brimming with filthy fantasies. I want to learn them all and make every single one come true. But this morning, I think I know what he needs, what he's been absolutely desperate for.

"I'm going to let go of your hands for a second, but don't move them," I tell him firmly, and he stops wiggling immediately, like he's trying to show me he understands and he's going to behave. Such a good boy.

My cock throbs against the hot skin of his thigh. I can't wait to be buried inside him, to feel his orgasm ripple through him, the clench of his inner muscles as I drive him to heights he's never known before. The very first fantasy he told me about was to have a Daddy make him come over and over, to *force* him to come even when he's sure he can't do it again, and that's exactly what I plan to give him this morning.

I release my hold on his hands and sit up, my thighs on either side of his. As horny as I am, this doesn't feel like a moment I want to rush. After all, it's the first time I'm playing with my boy in person, in my own bed. The warmth of his body, the scent of his sweat and precum, and the pink patches of skin on his chin that have already been rubbed slightly raw by my beard all imprint themselves on my mind.

His cock is a little shorter than average but nice and thick. If he's game for it, I'll pin him down and ride it hard one day. I love a good stretch, just the right amount of stinging fullness. I could tie him down and bounce up and down on his cock for hours, edging the hell out of both of us until I finally give in and cover him in my cum while he fills me with his.

My balls tighten at the thought, heat zinging through my body. Something to look forward to another day.

Emerson whines at being kept waiting, and I smirk. "Patience, sweetheart."

I run my hands over his chest, caressing his hard nipples with my thumbs and drawing a hiss from him. His cock jerks and spills a clear strand of precum onto his belly. He clenches his hands but keeps them over his head as he tries to hump up toward me, moaning when he realizes he's trapped by my body.

I reach over toward my bedside drawer. My plan was to grab the lube and the special toy I bought last week just for Emerson, but seeing his cock twitch and his body tremble from this hint of restraint, I grab my leather cuffs as well. A few weeks ago, we discussed both being negative and on PrEP, so I grab a condom and hold it up.

"Do you want me to use a condom? Just nod or shake your head."

Emerson shakes his head rapidly from side to side, so I drop the condom back into the drawer and set the rest of the items down on the bed. My boy is an absolute vision, all flushed and impatient, eyeing the things I pulled out and licking his lips.

I had the leather cuffs custom made years

ago, but I've never used them. I meant to, and in fact, I almost pulled them out on a few occasions with different boys, but something stopped me. There's just always been something about the lovely, intricate design etched into the buttery smooth leather that made them seem special, like I needed to save them for the right boy.

There isn't an ounce of hesitation inside me now as I fasten them around each wrist, making sure they're tight, but not so tight they'll cut off his circulation. Emerson pants and moans again as I clip the two cuffs together and then secure them to the connection point on my headboard. My bedframe is another thing I had custom made, with subtle connection points on both the headboard and footboard for all kinds of restraints.

His cock is absolutely gushing now, beckoning me to take a taste. I kiss his mouth first though, licking my way between his lips and swallowing the desperate sounds he feeds me, cherishing them as they vibrate against my tongue. I put one hand on his throat while I kiss him, not squeezing or cutting off his airway at all, just feeling his quickening pulse under my fingers and the bob of his Adam's apple when he swallows.

"Such a perfect boy," I murmur against his lips. "I was over the moon when I realized you were BraveBoy. I knew you were meant to be mine the first time I laid eyes on you."

Emerson melts under me, giving me delicious, happy sounds between each kiss. Eventually, I drag my lips down to his chin, along his throat, and over his chest and stomach until I near his cock. He bucks and groans, his cock bumping against my chin. I grin and keep kissing the rest of his body, dragging my beard against the inside of his thighs until they start to pink and then nibbling on his flesh, watching his cock jerk and weep. A few more wet kisses on his thighs and hips before I finally wrap my fingers around the base of his cock.

"I want to taste your cum. Be a good boy and give it to me." I swipe my tongue over the damp head of his erection and moan as the salty, sweet flavor of his precum lights up my taste buds.

Emerson gasps, his breath coming faster, harsher, his muscles all quivering as if he can feel my tongue on every inch of his skin. Humming hungrily, I wrap my lips around his slick, hot head, still laving my tongue over his slit to gather every drop of precum he feeds me.

The thickness of his cock is even more noticeable when my lips are stretched around his shaft, the weight of him resting against my tongue and pressing against the roof of my mouth. I barely have him halfway into my mouth when he lets out a low groan, his entire body tensing and then shuddering all at once as he fills my mouth with his bitter, sticky seed. I suck and lap at him, coaxing every drop I can out of him.

He's still hard but starting to soften when I release him from my mouth. He looks entirely and perfectly obscene, restrained with my pretty cuffs, his cock drenched with my spit and a few stray droplets of cum, milky and clinging to his shaft. Without taking my eyes off of the beautifully pornographic sight, I reach for the toy: a pretty purple vibrator with a nice, angled tip to hit his prostate just right.

I squirt a generous amount of lube onto it and then press it against his hole. Two nights ago, he sent me a short video of the dildo I had made for him stretching and fucking him until he splattered his phone with cum and the video ended. I know he could take my cock right now without much prep, but I'm not ready to finish playing with him just yet.

Emerson lets out a half moan, half startled gasp when I push the toy inside of him. His legs fall open, and his cock ceases softening, laying half-hard now.

"Such a naughty, horny boy. I think I'd better make sure you stock up on orgasms for the day," I say in a low, deep voice, using my knees to push his legs open wider as I fill him nice and deep with the toy.

He moans in response, nodding his head. I reflexively dart a glance at his fingers, making sure they're still their normal color, that the restraints aren't too tight while I tease him with the fullness of the toy for a second. His cock is slowly starting to harden again, not quite as desperate as the last time...yet. I use my thumb to turn on the vibrations.

Emerson jolts like he's being electrocuted, bucking his hips as his cock surges back to full hardness. I stop the vibration and then restart it, pulsing it against his prostate and watching the way his whole body rises and falls with each heavy breath he takes. He humps his cock up into the air, nearly sobbing when his second orgasm hits him, his cum splattering against his stomach.

I barely give him the chance to catch his breath before I'm pulling out the toy and replacing it with my cock, sliding easily into his relaxed, slick hole. I fill him in one thrust, groaning from deep in my gut when my thighs meet the back of his ass, every inch of my cock surrounded by the tight heat of him. I lean forward and kiss each one of his fingertips before swooping in and ravishing his mouth.

His cock isn't so quick to revive this time,

barely hard as I ease out and then thrust back in. He arches his body up against mine, seeking more of my touch. I do live to give my boy what he wants. I ease a little more of my weight onto him, kissing him deeply while I fuck him slowly.

Emerson sighs against my lips, dragging his tongue against mine as I tempt it out to play. I rock into him, filling him deep, and then staying there for a few beats before doing it all over again. Over and over while I lose track of time, lose track of everything other than Emerson. A bead of sweat trickles down my back, and his cock is starting to harden again.

I fuck him a little faster, my patience starting to fray as an urgency takes over. My balls are heavy, and my whole body is heating up. But I want to feel him come one more time before I do. I sit up and grab the lube, filling my palm and then wrapping my hand around his cock.

Emerson whines, shaking his head back and forth, the sensitivity no doubt almost too much.

"Unicorn?" I check, and he continues to shake his head. "Then give me one more."

He squirms like he can't decide if he wants more of my touch or not, giving in after a few seconds and humping into my fist. I look between us, my balls tightening at the sight of his hole stretched around my cock. Not a replica this time, but mine.

"I need it, sweetheart," I beg, so close to coming that my voice is tight and gruff.

Emerson nearly sobs, his cock pulsing dry in my hand, his inner muscles constricting around my cock and pushing me over the edge. I groan and fall forward, humping him desperately as I empty myself inside him. I drag my lips over his, not really kissing, but needing to taste him while my orgasm rolls through me.

I reach up and unclasp his hands, but stay on top of him, breathing him in and catching my breath long after I've started to soften and slip out. When my muscles start to tremble from the strain, I roll onto my side and pull Emerson close.

"You can talk again when you're ready," I murmur sleepily. I wonder what time it is and if I can convince my boy to stay a little longer, nap with me, and then enjoy a leisurely brunch together. My housekeeper optimistically left a quiche for me when I mentioned I had a big date this weekend.

"Wow," he says breathily, a weak smile dancing over his lips.

"Me too," I agree, pressing a kiss to the top of his head. "Stay a little while?"

He nods his head and wiggles closer, making himself comfortable.

"Em?" I ask, and he hums in response. "Why did you lie about the tattoo when I asked before?"

A slightly guilty expression replaces the serene one. "It's em-em-embarrassing."

"What?" I laugh, running my hand down to his backside and squeezing the cheek that I know has the pretty little ink on it. "It's not embarrassing, it's cute."

He snorts and shakes his head and then rests it against my chest and closes his eyes, falling asleep almost instantly.

I lie awake, running my fingers slowly up and down his spine and making a mental list of all the ways I'm *not* going to fuck this one up.

CHAPTER 16

Emerson

The second time I wake up in Kiernan's bed, there's dry cum crusted on my skin, and I'm all alone. Ugh, I *definitely* preferred the first wake-up. I yawn and rub my eyes, a bit of a sleep hangover making me feel groggy and stupid. What time is it? What *day* is it? And oh my god, how do I have to pee *this* badly?

I throw back the covers and hurry to the en-suite bathroom to relieve my bladder. Once that's handled, I find a clean rag and get it wet in the sink so I can hastily clean myself up a bit. The bathroom is huge, big enough to echo. The acoustics for shower singing must be insane, or even better...sex. I wander over to the massive tub and take a peek at all of the bombs and salts that are lined up along the edge. I figured he was just trying to pamper me with the box of goodies he sent, but it's clear that Kiernan is a man who likes his luxury bath products. I strongly approve.

"Sweetheart?" There's a gentle knock at the

bathroom door, a smile jumping instantly to my lips at the sound of Kiernan's voice.

I scurry over and open the door, flinging myself into his arms. He lets out an *oomph* but catches me with ease. Sadly, at some point while I was sleeping, he put on a pair of sweatpants and a T-shirt. I have to admit that there's something erotic about being all naked in his arms while he has clothes on.

"M-mmm-morning," I say, grinning as I wrap myself around him like a spider monkey.

"Good morning." He tightens his arms around me and presses a soft kiss to my lips. "Did you find everything you needed in the bathroom?"

"Toothbrush?" I ask hopefully, embarrassed for the first time that the man practically licked my tonsils earlier without any regard for my dragon breath.

"I can get you one. But I have breakfast if you'd rather eat first."

I tilt my head to look past him and see a tray resting on the bed with all kinds of delicious foods—quiche, muffins, an array of fruit... there even seems to be both coffee *and* tea on the nightstand.

All of my insides start to feel mushy. He didn't know if I liked coffee or tea, so he brought both. Fuck my morning breath, I tighten my arms around his neck and kiss him. All of this might be new to me, but I'm going to be the best boy in the entire world so he'll want to keep me forever. I can be perfect for him. I *have* to be perfect for him.

My heart beats a little hard, and not in a good way, as I realize I'm not exactly sure *how* to be the perfect boy. What if I mess everything up? What if he finds a boy who doesn't have any issues saying the words on his mind whenever he wants to say them? What if he gets bored with me?

"Shh, Brave Boy," he murmurs against my lips. "What's wrong?"

My throat tightens, and my tongue feels too heavy, so I give a sharp shake of my head instead. I'm not totally sure how to be a perfect boy...*yet*, but I don't think it involves babbling a bunch of stuttered insecurities at Daddy when he's thoughtful enough to bring me breakfast in bed.

I wiggle until Kiernan loosens his grip, and then I slide down his body, putting my feet on the floor again. He drags his eyes over my bare body, heat filling his expression, and I preen a little. I wonder if Daddy is going to have rules and if being naked can be one of them. Am I allowed to ask for a rule? Maybe once I have some coffee in me, I'll be brave enough to find out. I grab his hand and pull him over to the bed, careful not to spill the tray as I climb on and get myself settled. He follows suit, and within a couple of minutes, we both have our own mug of steaming coffee and we're nibbling on breakfast.

"Muffin for your thoughts?" he asks, offering me a bite-size blueberry muffin.

I smile and take it, popping it into my mouth and gathering up my courage to answer his question. "Do I g-g-get rules?"

"You do. Do you want your rules now?" he asks, and I nod rapidly. Once I have rules, I'll know this is *really* real, that Kiernan truly wants to be my Daddy. "I'll tell you what, I'll write up a list of rules for you today, and then I can give them to you on our date tomorrow night."

He says it so casually, but I swear there's the barest hint of vulnerability in his voice. As if I would turn down a date with him. Doesn't he know I would do anything for him?

"Okay," I agree with a smile. I want to ask where he's going to take me, but if he wants me to know, he'll tell me on his own. I trust him. With that in mind, I manage to find the words I needed a few minutes ago. "C-c-c-can I ask for a rule?"

"You can ask." He studies me, taking a sip

of his coffee.

"I want to be n-n-n-naked wh-wh-when we're alone." I hold my breath after I get the words out. The request is relatively tame compared to some of the things I told him as BraveBoy, but it's the first time I've asked for something like this aloud. He teased that I'm a dirty boy, and it sounded like a good thing at the time, but what if I'm *too* horny. Should a good boy be more virginal? Sterling certainly comes across as shy and Barrett seems into it.

"Mm, that's an excellent rule," he agrees, easing some of my worries. "We'll have to talk about consequences for breaking rules too."

"I w-won't," I promise him quickly. *I'll be the perfect boy*; I assure myself again.

"Of course I want you to follow the rules, sweetheart, but sometimes a little bit of purposeful misbehavior can be part of the scene for a boy."

I blink at him in horror. I know about brats, and I guess I was a little feisty last night for fun, but it's hard for me to understand why a boy would purposefully disobey his Daddy. The question must be written all over my face.

"Some boys misbehave because they enjoy punishments, or *funishments,* as some people call them," he explains with a wink. "Sometimes they misbehave to test their boundaries or to see how serious their Daddy is about the rules."

"Hmm," I hum thoughtfully. "I'll be good," I say again, and he leans over the food tray and kisses me, the taste of coffee and blueberries lingering on both of our mouths.

I'm tempted to text Sterling to ask if he can cover the shop by himself this afternoon and then beg Kiernan to let me stay here naked in his bed for the rest of the day. But, if I don't go in, I won't get the chance to ask Sterling the million and one questions currently buzzing through my head about all the ways to be the absolute most perfect boy who ever lived.

When Kiernan pulls back, he drags his thumb gently along my bottom lip. "You still have a little bit of lipstick," he explains, showing me the bit of red clinging to the pad of his thumb.

"Did you l-l-like me wearing it?" I didn't mind it much, except that the stickiness felt a bit strange. I'm sure I could get used to it.

"I like you feeling comfortable and sexy," he answers. "If that means wearing makeup, then I'll buy you all the makeup you want. If it means being completely and utterly bare from head to toe, then I'll make sure the house is always the perfect temperature."

My heart flutters happily. Is Kiernan even

real, or is this some wild, incredible dream that I'll wake up from any second? If it's the latter, I hope I sleep for a *very* long time.

Kiernan

It's such a shame when Emerson finally has to get dressed so I can drive him home in time to go open his store. But there's not much that can dampen my mood after such an incredible morning and the promise of a date tomorrow night.

My mind is already spinning over all the ways I can impress my boy tomorrow night as I pull up in front of his apartment. I park the car in front of his building and unbuckle so I can turn toward him. He unfastens his seatbelt as well, nibbling on his bottom lip and giving me an absurdly shy look for a man who was comfortably naked in my bed not half an hour ago. I grin and lean over to brush a kiss to his lips. He sighs and leans in, too greedy for the brief good-bye kiss I intended.

"You have to go to work," I remind him, stealing another few pecks from his lips before he leans back and makes a frustrated sound in the back of his throat.

"C-can I c-c-call you later?" he asks, fiddling with the door handle but not actually opening the door.

"You can call me any time you want, sweetheart," I say, and he nods, still looking uncertain. "I mean it. If you wake up at two in the morning and just need to hear my voice, you call. If you're at work an hour from now and want to call me for reassurance that all of this is real, pick up the phone and make the call. I know this is all new, but the first and most important thing I need you to know is that I'm here for you, *always*."

The smile that spreads over his lips rivals the brightest sunshine.

"How about if I j-just c-c-call when I close the shop at s-s-ss-seven?" he asks in a teasing tone.

"Sounds like a plan," I agree, resisting the urge to pull him onto my lap for one more kiss, or a few hundred more if I had my way. "Have a good day."

"Yes, Daddy," Emerson says sweetly before finally getting out of the car. I watch as he heads inside, and then I wait a few moments longer until I see the blinds in his apartment window sway. I can't see well enough from down here, but I think he's peeking to see if I'm still here. *Always, baby*.

It's late enough in the day that I've already

missed the regular brunch my friends and I take turns hosting, but if I remember correctly, it's Alden's turn this week, and I would bet that Barrett and his sister, Lorna, are still over there, enjoying too many Bloody Marys and speculating about what happened between me and Emerson last night.

Sure enough, when I pull up, I see the expected extra cars in Alden's large driveway. I park behind Lorna's custom pink Jag and make my way inside, not bothering to knock.

I follow the sound of voices down the long hallway to the kitchen, where I find my friends congregated, the half-empty pitcher of Bloody Marys on the counter.

"Didn't expect to see you today," Alden says as soon as he notices me in the entrance to the kitchen. "You missed the food, but come in and pour yourself a drink."

I bypass the alcohol and help myself to a glass of orange juice instead, intensely aware of three sets of eyes boring into me.

Lorna is the first to break. "You and that sweet little Emerson looked awfully lost in each other's eyes last night," she notes with a hint of amusement.

"To put it mildly," Alden offers helpfully.

"Yeah, how exactly did that happen? Last

we all heard you had some new boy you were excited about." Barrett's expression is by far the most critical when I finally turn to face the group, taking a sip of my orange juice and leaning against the counter.

"Yes," I agree. "Emerson is my new boy."

Lorna makes a rather pleased sound while Alden tilts his head, continuing to study me, and Barrett frowns.

"And the boy from M4M?" Alden asks, for once not sounding at all bored with the conversation.

"That was Em. It was always Em." I mean that in more ways than one. It was *always* Emerson. Before I knew he existed, somehow it was still Emerson.

"That's the most romantic thing I've ever heard," Lorna sighs, putting a hand over her heart. "I need to find a new baby girl to play with."

"There's a woman at my gym who's just your type. Shall I slip her your number the next time I see her?" Alden offers, and Barrett makes an impatient sound.

"Can we focus for a second? I'm sure Lorna's quest for a new girl can wait five minutes."

"Ah yes, lecturing me, a grown adult entering into a relationship with another consenting adult, should certainly take priority," I say dryly.

"I'm not going to lecture you, but Em is Sterling's best friend, so if I don't do my due diligence here and the boy ends up hurt, I'll never hear the end of it."

"I'm not going to hurt him," I insist.

"He's not really your usual type." Alden with another classic assist.

"Right," I huff. "My usual type is over-primped gold-diggers who figure the fastest way to my wallet is through my dick. Emerson isn't experienced in the lifestyle, but he's not a naïve child either."

"No one is calling him a child," Barrett assures me.

"Great, so if you recognize that Emerson is adult enough to know what he wants, and I've always proven myself to be respectful to the boys I play with, even the ones who are greedy users, then I guess we don't have a problem," I say coolly.

Barrett stares me down for a few seconds while Lorna darts nervous looks between the two of us, like she's trying to figure out what she'll do if this comes to blows. For all of Alden's previous interest, he seems to have gotten bored with the subject and is now texting and sipping his drink without much care.

"I guess we don't," Barrett finally agrees.

With that settled, we return to the topic of where Lorna might go on the hunt for someone to play with. I'm only half-listening while I pull out my phone and order a large bouquet of roses to send to Unicorn Books for Emerson, as well as a few other little trinkets to surprise him with tomorrow night. A nice pair of gold cufflinks should make a nice gift.

Barrett sidles up next to me, and I put my phone away.

"I was never questioning you as a Daddy Dom," he says softly. I bristle a little, ready to tell him that I was never worried about his approval, except maybe I was. Just a little. Not his *approval*, but hearing another Daddy Dom question me, someone I'm as close with as Barrett, isn't sitting well.

"You know I always take care of my boys."

"I know you do," he agrees.

"And you know I'll take care of Emerson."

"Yes, I do know that. I was just looking out for *my* boy. He really cares about Em. Sterling says he's the first real friend he's ever had. You can imagine why I'd feel a little protective."

"I understand, and I appreciate that, but

Emerson is mine to worry about now."

He takes a sip from his drink and nods. "Understood. No hard feelings?"

"No hard feelings." I clasp his shoulder and give it an affectionate squeeze.

My phone buzzes in my pocket, and I pull it out to find a text from Emerson about a book he's setting aside for me. I smile, my heart feeling full and light all at once. I may have fucked up in the past, chosen the wrong boys and looked for love in the wrong places, but this feels different. Maybe I'm getting ahead of myself, but Emerson feels different than anyone else. He feels like mine, and I'm going to make sure he stays that way.

CHAPTER 17

Emerson

Sterling didn't turn out to be a ton of help on the *perfect boy* front. He kept saying stuff like "be yourself" and "Kiernan already wants to be your Daddy, just relax." Ugh, it's like he doesn't realize what's at stake here. But if he wants to keep all of his secrets to himself, then fine. I figure I can learn to be Kiernan's perfect boy all on my own. Which led me down a Google rabbit hole well past midnight.

Being all tired and puffy eyed isn't how I was hoping to spend my first official date with Daddy Kiernan, but it's nothing a little caffeine and concealer can't fix. Nothing is going to get me down tonight because *it's my first official date with Daddy Kiernan*. I barely manage to keep myself from squealing aloud. I don't think my neighbor would appreciate that, although he's certainly heard much worse from my side of the wall.

I check the time while I dab a bit of concealer under my eye to cover up the bags. I grin and wiggle my butt excitedly. Daddy is going to be here any minute, and I seriously can't wait. I've been daydreaming all day about what he has planned for tonight. I'm sure he's going to take me somewhere super fancy, but part of me hopes it'll be somewhere more romantic and lowkey instead. I'd rather take a picnic to a duck pond and feed the ducks while we eat and talk than go to some million-star restaurant with tiny portions and weird sauces.

A knock at my door has me jumping with excitement and nerves, nearly dropping the bottle of concealer onto the carpet. I catch it just in time, my hands shaking badly enough that it takes me a few tries to get the cap on before I hurry to answer the door.

I pause in front of the hallway mirror, taking a deep breath and mentally running through the things I found online last night, the proper way to kneel for a Dom being at the top of my list of ways to impress Kiernan tonight.

I may have a difficult time with my words, but that doesn't mean I can't show Kiernan how much I want him as my Daddy. With one more deep breath, I pull open the door and nearly lose my breath at the sight of the gorgeous, impossibly handsome man in front of me. His hair is tamed today, but his beard is just as wild as always. I instinctively clench my legs together, still feeling a hint of beard burn on the insides of my thighs from the other morning. He's wearing a navy-blue suit today, the top few buttons on his button-up shirt undone to reveal the soft, thick hair on his chest.

"Hi, Daddy," I say breathlessly, licking my lips. I want to launch myself into his arms like I did the other morning, but instead I drop to my knees, putting my hands behind my back and ducking my head, just like I saw in all of the pictures.

Kiernan gasps, and to my surprise, lifts me off the floor and into his arms. "Sweetheart, these floors are wood. You're going to hurt yourself dropping like that without any padding."

A hint of shame tightens around my chest. This isn't how it was supposed to go. I thought Daddy Kiernan would be happy to see me kneeling for him. I wrap my arms and legs around him and let him carry me into the living room, frowning as I try to work out where I went wrong.

He sits down on the couch, taking me with him onto his lap, and then runs his thumb along my bottom lip, a concerned expression on his face.

"I want to be p-p-p-perfect for you."

"Oh, sweet boy, I don't need you bruising up your knees to be perfect for me. If you want to kneel for me, we can add that to your rules, but it's not something I need from you." He runs his fingers gently through my hair, and I lean into his touch, closing my eyes and trying to sort through how I'm feeling. If Daddy doesn't want me to kneel for him, what about the other things I saw last night like licking his shoes? I wasn't so sure about that one, but I figured his shoes look pretty clean usually so it shouldn't be *too* bad. How will I know how to be the perfect boy for him?

He must read the conflict on my face, or maybe he's just so amazing he knows exactly what I'm thinking. "You don't have to worry so much. It's my job as your Daddy to *tell* you what I need you to do. If you're confused or uncertain of how to act, that's my fault, not yours."

I scrunch my eyebrows together, sifting through what he's saying. All I have to do to be a good boy for him is to do what he says? That seems almost too easy.

"Really?" I ask, cocking my head and searching his face for any sign that this is some kind of test.

"Really." He rubs a hand up and down my back, and I relax into his touch. "In fact, why don't I give you your rules now so you know exactly how you can be a good boy for me."

I nod eagerly, letting him shift me so he can reach into his pocket. He pulls out a piece of paper and hands it to me.

Kiernan

Emerson unfolds the paper, straddling me with his legs on either side of mine. I put my hands on his thighs and jerk my chin toward the paper. "Read that for me, Brave Boy, and then you can tell me if you have any questions."

He nods again, licking his lips as his eyes scan down the list. "O-one," he reads. "Emerson must go to sleep at ten o'clock every night." He stops and scowls.

"You need your rest," I say sternly before he can argue. "You stay up too late and you're tired all day."

He huffs through his nose but keeps reading. "Two: Emerson m-mmm-must eat lunch, even if work is busy." I get another stink eye and fight back the urge to smile at how fucking cute he looks when he's annoyed. "I thought these w-w-would be s-s-s-ss-sexy rules," he grumbles.

"Making sure my boy is well taken care of is *very* sexy," I reason. "Keep reading."

"Three: Emerson must be naked at Daddy's house unless otherwise instructed." This time he grins. "N-n-now we're talking."

I chuckle. "What are your other rules?" I

prompt, and he keeps reading.

"Four: All of Emerson's orgasms belong to Daddy." His breath hitches and a dirty smile spreads over his lips, but he keeps going. "Five: Emerson must spend at least one n-night per week in Daddy's bed."

He looks up from the list, and I brush his hair off his forehead. Up close like this, I notice some puffiness to his eyes, proving my point of how necessary the first rule is. My boy isn't great at sleeping like he should. But that's okay because I'm here to take care of him now.

"I thought five was a good start, and we can add to it as we feel is necessary. Okay?" I check, and he nods. "What questions do you have?"

"C-can I always call you Daddy? Even in public?"

"If you're comfortable, then I would love that," I assure him, pressing a kiss to his cheek because the pink blush blooming there is too pretty to resist.

He nods and then squirms a little on my lap, waking up my cock as he nibbles on his bottom lip shyly. "I...I mm-m-made you a list too."

I raise both of my eyebrows, an amused smirk tugging at the corners of my lips. "Rules for Daddy?" I ask, and Emerson's eyes go wide in horror.

"N-n-n-n…"

"Relax, sweetheart, it's okay," I assure him, squeezing his thighs and kissing him again, on the lips this time to reassure him. "What kind of list did you make me?"

His blush deepens to a full-on crimson. There's such a fascinating dichotomy between the filthy things he said to me in our chats and how shy he comes across in real life. He just needs time to trust me, then I have no doubt he'll get comfortable enough to say all of the dirty things aloud that I know he's thinking.

Emerson shuffles off of my lap and picks up a notebook off of the little table next to the couch. He flips it open and hands it to me. I guess it's my turn to read aloud.

"*Emerson's Fantasies*," I read from the page, my cock swelling further, creating a bulge in the front of my suit pants. "Interesting." I grab my boy and pull him back onto my lap, scanning the list quickly and sensing a theme: sex on his balcony where someone might hear, sex in an elevator, crawling under my desk at work to pleasure me with his mouth, being naked at a kink club… "For a sweet, shy boy, there's an awful lot of exhibitionism on this list," I tease lightly, and he makes a nervous sound in his throat, ducking his head to hide his face in the crook of my neck.

"Number four is certainly interesting. You want me to pick out something pretty for you to wear and then take you to a kink club. I happen to be a member of one right outside of town, although, granted, I haven't been in a while. What would we consider pretty, Brave Boy?"

He shrugs, slowly showing me his face again, his bottom lip puffy from the abuse of his teeth. "A-anything Daddy says."

"It sounds like we have a plan for our second date then." I tear the list out and fold it up to put into my pocket for future reference. Emerson's expression lights up, and he bobbles his head eagerly. "Perfect. But first, we have *tonight's* date to attend to. I have reservations at *Le Petite Maison*."

Emerson's smile falters for a second before it comes back full force. He puts both hands on my chest and smiles. "I d-don't care where we eat as l-l-long as I'm with you."

Fuck, could he be any sweeter? I drag him in for another kiss, longer and deeper this time. Our reservation will keep for a few minutes. Right now, I want to make out on the couch with my boy like teenagers, and he doesn't seem to have any objections.

This could be the real thing. It feels like it is. I hope he feels it too.

CHAPTER 18

Emerson

I flit around my kitchen, gathering snacks and drinks, smiling to myself at the sound of all of my friends in the living room. Well, mostly the sound of Sterling and Nolan, but Gannon is out there too, silent but ever present. From the sound of it, Sterling is trying to explain to Nolan exactly what the appeal of getting a spanking is.

I'm not sure if I would like a spanking. Is it a given when you have a Daddy? I itch to reach for my phone and do a little research—my fallback past time, clearly—but then I remember that Kiernan said the only thing I need to do to be his perfect boy is whatever he says. If Daddy wants to spank me, he can. Until then, I won't worry about it.

There's a pep in my step as I carry the tray of goodies into the living room. It really is amazing what a consistent good night's sleep can do for a person. I thought that going to bed early would put a crimp in my writing time, but I've been waking up fresh enough each morning to get words in before going to open the bookstore. Daddy's so smart.

"I don't know. I'm just not sure I'd like a man telling me what to do all the time. Even if the sex was bomb," Nolan says with a shrug.

Sterling shakes his head like the man is talking crazy, and I just smile and blush. Having a Daddy probably isn't for everyone, but damn am I happy I found Kiernan...or he found me. I'm not sure which it is. Maybe we found each other. Either way, I'm never letting him go.

"S-s-snacks," I declare happily, setting the tray down with a flourish. My friends all help themselves, and I make myself comfortable with a big smile on my face. It's hard to believe how much has changed in the past year since Sterling walked into Unicorn Books, all shy and insecure about the birthmark on his face. I had no idea how good of friends we would become or that he'd introduce me to Kiernan. More than that, he's shown me what it feels like to truly belong somewhere.

"What are you smilin' about?" he asks, noticing my attention on him.

"Just glad we're f-friends," I admit.

"Aw, me too." He leans over in his chair and kisses my cheek.

Sometime later, when the snacks are gone

and we've covered so many different conversation topics that I've completely lost track, there's a knock at my door.

"Ooh, I bet that's your Daddy," Sterling says, waggling his eyebrows.

Heat floods through me, my stomach giving an excited flutter as I jump up and go to find out if he's right. I can't imagine who else it would be, other than maybe my neighbor coming to tell me that we're being too loud. Living in an apartment is annoying.

But nope, no irritated neighbor, just my sexy as fuck Daddy.

"Hey, beautiful," he greets me with a slow smirk, leaning down to press a soft, addicting kiss to my lips.

"Hi, Daddy."

The sound of Nolan's laughter echoes down the hall. "I'm sorry. I didn't know you had friends over. Should I call you later instead?"

"N-n-no." I answer quickly, grabbing his hand and pulling him inside. "I l-love surprise visits."

"Glad to hear it." I can hear a hint of amusement in his tone. Maybe due to my enthusiasm as I drag him toward the living room.

"I have another surprise for you as well."

As soon as we stop, he reaches into his pocket and pulls out a sleek black box. My eyes go wide, and I dart a glance toward my friends, all looking over curiously.

"It's n-n-n-n..." My tongue gets clumsy, and I grunt in frustration.

"It's safe to open," Daddy assures me with a wink. I didn't *think* he'd give me a sex toy in front of other people, but I did just give him a list of fantasies that were pretty heavily skewed toward liking to give people a show. I'd just like a little bit of warning and maybe *some* choice of my audience before going ahead with all of that.

I take the box and carefully flip the lid open. My mouth falls open at the sight of it. I think a sex toy would've been far less shocking actually.

"Holy shit," Nolan mutters.

"Shiny," Sterling adds.

Gannon grunts. I can't tell if it's a compliment or a judgment.

"Do you like it?" Kiernan asks.

"I...um..." I stare at the diamond encrusted watch. It's not exactly practical if I'm being honest. Okay, it's more than impractical; it's downright gaudy. It must've cost an absolute fortune. Damn, Daddy's waiting for my answer, and I'm being rude. I force a smile, my whole face feeling tight. "It's b-b-b-..." I stop and lick my lips. "It's nice."

Kiernan frowns, and I hurry to put the watch on, hoping that will sell my enthusiasm for the gift. I love that he thought of me, but is there a nice way to tell him that a present like this was completely unnecessary?

"Maybe we should go," Sterling says, standing up. Nolan and Gannon follow suit.

"You don't have to," I try to reassure them. If they stay a little longer, maybe it will give me time to figure out how to respond to the gift before I'm alone with Kiernan and he asks again if I like it. Fuck, I'm such a bad liar. Plus, I really don't *want* to lie to Daddy.

"Sterling's right; it's getting late," Nolan agrees.

I tug my bottom lip between my teeth and nod reluctantly. "I'll sh-sh-show you out."

Kiernan makes himself comfortable in the living room while I walk my friends to the door. "What do I d-do?" I whisper frantically to Sterling. We both look at the heavy, disco ball-looking watch.

"You hate it?" he asks just as quietly, and I nod. "Tell him the truth. The truth is always better than a lie."

"Fuck," I mutter, afraid that was going to

be the answer.

"Good luck," Nolan whispers. "And if you need to get rid of the watch, my birthday is coming up." He winks before Gannon snorts and shakes his head, steering Nolan out.

I stand in the hallway an extra few seconds, gathering my courage before dragging my feet back to the living room, pasting another awkward smile on.

"D-d-d-d-do you w-w-want a d-d-d-drink?" I manage to stutter out the question, my mouth feeling clumsy as my hands sweat and my stomach knots. What if Daddy is mad that I don't like it? What if he thinks I'm ungrateful? I don't want to hurt his feelings.

"I'm fine. Come here, sweetheart." He crooks a finger to beckon me over, and I gather up all my courage to crawl onto his lap.

Kiernan

I thought the watch would be a slam dunk. I spent an hour at the jeweler picking out the Phillipe Patek and then imagined the look on Emerson's face the entire drive over. Except, the expression he had when he opened it wasn't at all what I'd been imagining. He looked... uncomfortable.

"You hate it," I say as soon as my boy is on

my lap.

He shakes his head, blushing, and then grimaces and nods slowly. "I r-r-really appreciate it, it's j-j-just not m-m-mm-me."

He's practically shaking as he holds his wrist out awkwardly, like if he looks at the watch at just the right angle, he'll start to like it.

"Shh, it's okay." I rub a hand up and down his back to soothe him. "It's fine if you don't like it. Tell me what you *would* like, and it's yours. Would you prefer a watch without diamonds? Or something else entirely? How about a new car? A trip somewhere nice?"

Emerson blinks at me a few times like he's trying to solve a puzzle and then leans in and kisses me so softly on the lips that it's barely there, yet, I can feel it all the way to my toes at the same time.

"Daddy, I d-don't need *things*." He takes the watch off and carefully hands it back to me. "I only need you."

His words hit me right in the center of my chest, stealing my breath in an instant. My throat tightens, and I'm not sure if I want to laugh or cry. Of course he doesn't need to be showered in the same expensive, elaborate gifts that other boys I've dated wanted, because he's not like them. He's not dating me for my money or status.

I take the watch from him and slip it into my pocket, wrapping both arms around him and hugging him close. "You are an absolute treasure, my perfect, sweet boy." I murmur, pressing kisses all along his face and down his neck. He laughs and squirms and then goes still and moans when I gently nip at the fluttering pulse point in his throat.

"If you w-want to give me presents, more n-naughty toys are good," he offers breathlessly, and I chuckle against his neck, sucking a patch of skin just above his collarbone until he gasps and bucks against me. I wonder which category a collar would fall into.

I've never collared a boy before, but damn if I can't get the thought of my sweet little Emerson in a soft, leather collar out of my mind.

"I'll keep that in mind," I promise, cupping him by the back of the neck and covering his mouth with mine.

My boy melts into the kiss, opening for me eagerly and dragging his tongue against mine, hot and wet and tempting as hell.

I stand up without warning, taking him with me. Emerson gasps into my mouth, hurrying to wrap his arms and legs around me...as if I'd ever drop him.

"B-bedroom?" he guesses breathlessly between kisses.

"Balcony," I correct with a wicked grin against his mouth.

He lets out a desperate, horny sound and grinds his hardening cock against me.

Once I step through the sliding door to his balcony, I break the kiss so I can get the lay of the land. It's fairly small with a steel railing. There's just enough room for a ratty-looking chaise lounge and for maybe two people to stand simultaneously. Not enough space for a party, but more than enough room for what I have in mind.

"Hmm," I hum, peeking over the edge, still holding Emerson in my arms. "We're only on the second floor. It would be easy for someone to catch a glimpse of us up here if they got curious."

He moans again, his cock twitching. My boy really does like the idea of being seen, doesn't he? I drag my beard over the soft skin of his throat, delighting in the easy pinking of his skin.

"Do you want someone to see how much you love having your throat stuffed with Daddy's cock?"

He groans and bobs his head, humping and thrusting against me while trying to wiggle out of my arms at the same time, clearly eager to take what I'm offering him. "P-please," he pants.

I kiss him again, greedy for the taste of his mouth. He relaxes against me, like putty in my arms, except for the one *very* hard part of him I can still feel.

My own cock is thick and throbbing, rubbing against the soft fabric of my underwear and growing harder by the second. I swear I can feel every swipe of his tongue all the way in the tip of my cock. He's so sweet and eager, so unbelievably hungry for everything I want to give him.

The sound of a car door opening and closing from the parking lot below causes Emerson to still in my arms. I grin against his lips, breaking the kiss and setting him down. He glances over the side of the flimsy railing and then back at me, nervous excitement dancing in his expression.

I unzip my pants slowly, shoving the front down just enough to pull my cock out while a set of voices reaches us from below. Can they see us? Unlikely unless they're looking. Will they hear us? Maybe. Is the possibility turning my boy the fuck on? Without a doubt. His cheeks darken, and his breath quickens, his hand landing on the bulge in the front of his pants.

"Come over here and be a good boy for Daddy," I purr, giving my cock a few slow strokes until a drop of precum beads on the slit, tempting my boy closer.

He lowers himself to his knees, thankfully more carefully than he did the other night, and shuffles closer. Emerson looks better than any wet dream I've ever had, looking up at me with so much eager hunger in his eyes, his lips damp and parted, intense awe coloring every inch of his expression. Is it too soon to be in love with him? Not that the answer to that matters. Either way, I'm pretty sure I already am.

I cup his jaw in one hand, the other still wrapped around the base of my cock. He closes his eyes and leans into my touch when I trace my thumb along his bottom lip and then shove it into his mouth.

"Look at me," I instruct gently, his eyes popping open instantly. "Good boy."

Ecstasy flashes over his expression, his eyelids fluttering but remaining open, his whole body shuddering like those two simple words gave him a full-body orgasm. I push my thumb against his tongue, my cock pulsing in my grip at the pillowy-soft, scorching hot heaven of his mouth.

The voices below continue, Emerson's breath hitching at each tendril of laughter that reaches us. "They're going to hear you choke on my cock. Are you ready?"

He nods, his teeth scraping against my

thumb. He whines when I pull my thumb out but settles when I rest the head of my cock against his lips as a replacement.

His mouth is soft and pliant as I rub my cock along his lips like lipstick, leaving a trail of sticky precum shining on them. He darts his tongue out and moans, opening even wider and hitting me with puppy dog eyes, begging me to stick it in already. I consider teasing, making him beg for it, but I'm not really in the mood to deny my boy anything. I push inside and groan loudly as the heat of his mouth engulfs me.

The voices below quiet for a second. I guess they *can* hear us up here. Emerson trembles and takes me deeper, making a hungry sound that vibrates down my shaft and settles in my balls.

"Do you think they know you're a dirty boy?" I ask, my voice strained as I hold still with my cock deep in his throat. Each breath he takes through his nose ghosts over my knuckles still wrapped around my base so he doesn't take too much too fast. "Or do you think they're jealous of you?"

He whines, lapping his tongue along my shaft. "Show them what a good little cocksucker you are."

Emerson moans again, grabbing onto my ass and pulling me deeper. I release my hold on my cock, burying my fingers in his hair and throwing my head back with a low, deep, "*Fuuuuuuck.*"

He sucks and licks and takes every inch of my substantial length as if it's the very air he needs to breathe. He makes obscene, sloppy, ball-tingling sounds while keeping his eyes locked on mine. It's like he's in the cock-sucking Olympics, and he refuses to go home with anything but a gold medal.

My hips twitch, heat creeping up my spine as Emerson bobs his head faster. I don't do anything to muffle the sounds he drags out of me, aware that he's getting off on knowing his neighbors might hear.

"I'm going to come, sweetheart," I grit out, fucking into his throat shamelessly. Each time he swallows, all of the muscles constrict around my cock and tighten my balls. With a loud groan, I spill down his throat, and my boy greedily laps up every drop I feed him, sucking me until my cock starts to soften.

I tighten my hands in his hair and pry him off of my cock, earning a whine in return.

"Come here," I say gently, pulling my pants back into place and tucking my cock away, and then sitting down on the chair. Emerson scrambles to join me, lying mostly on top of me so we both fit. I can feel his heartbeat slowing along with my own. I'll take him inside and return the favor by making him come soon. But first I want to enjoy the nice, quiet night with him for a few minutes.

The voices are gone now. Whether scared off by the sounds we were making or not, I'm not sure, nor do I care.

"Tell me something," I request, holding my boy against me and hoping that this chair on his balcony is sturdier than it looks. He closes his eyes and nestles closer.

"Mm-my favorite book growing up was *Alice in W-Wonderland*."

"Oh yeah?" I stroke my fingers through his hair. "I've seen the movie, but I haven't read it. Will you tell me about it?"

He smiles and does just that, telling me not only about *Alice in Wonderland* but going on to talk about a dozen other books he read when he was young.

"B-b-b-books never judge," he says, absently stroking his fingers up and down my chest. "They were the p-perfect escape when everything else felt too judgmental and awful."

I kiss the top of his head. "Kids can be assholes."

"Adults too," he says, his voice dripping with sadness that I know I can't just kiss away, as much as I'd love to.

We lie just like that until we both lose track of time, talking about everything and nothing. I could listen to him talk all night, all week...forever if he'll let me.

CHAPTER 19

Emerson

I squirm impatiently on Kiernan's bed, naked from head to toe and just a little bit obsessed with how soft his sheets are.

"Daddy," I complain.

The only answer I get is a deep, throaty chuckle from inside his enormous walk-in closet. Seriously, I'm pretty sure the thing is bigger than my whole apartment.

It's been a few weeks since I gave him my list of fantasies, and tonight, when I came over to his house, he told me we were going to Ball and Chain, the kink club right outside the city that he's a member of. Then he told me to strip down and disappeared into that damn closet. I told him he could dress me, not torture me by making me sit *patiently* for approximately an eternity.

I drum my fingers against the bed, which fails to have any kind of dramatic effect since it doesn't produce any sound. My stomach dances with a combination of nerves and excitement.

I've played out this fantasy a hundred times. Hell, I've written some version of it into at least a dozen books. But now that it's coming true, I can't seem to make myself stop trembling.

Kiernan finally steps out of the closet dressed in a pair of leather pants, a matching harness on his chest that he's covering as he buttons up a crisp, white shirt. My mouth falls open at the way the pants hug his thick thighs.

"Daddy," I say again, this time with lustful awe rather than impatience.

"Do you like it?" he checks, and I nod eagerly. "Good. I have something for you now."

I don't notice the bag in his hand until he holds it out to me. I scramble onto my knees and take it from him, peeking inside and bouncing with excitement as I pull out a harness that looks like it matches his and a pair of leather shorts that are barely more than underwear.

"C-can I put them on?"

"In a second." He crawls onto the bed, hovering over me with a predatory smile that sends happy shivers all through my body. My cock reacts immediately, perking up as my breath speeds up at the same time. "We need to discuss limits for tonight."

Limits? Is he planning to fuck me at the club in front of people? My cock swells and aches, and a moan slips past my lips. Kiernan smirks at me, and I'm starting to think he really can read my mind. Or maybe it's just super obvious that I'm *always* thinking something dirty.

"A-anything," I answer breathlessly, arching up to feel more of his body against mine. His leather pants are so smooth on my skin that I can't help but thrust shamelessly against him a few times.

He chuckles again, a warm, sweet look in his eyes as he drags his fingers through my hair and kisses one cheek, then the other, and then a soft touch of his lips to mine. "Not anything, Brave Boy. Not the first time anyway."

"S-s-s-sss-so we can go again?" I ask hopefully.

"We haven't even gone once yet," he points out with a smirk. "Back to the topic. Would you feel comfortable being naked?"

I nod rapidly, thrusting up against his leather-clad thigh again, my cock getting harder, stiffer, needier, as I imagine being dressed in the harness and shorts, my erection freed and swinging openly for anyone to see. I want perfect strangers lusting after me, unable to look away, and I want to know that Kiernan is the only one who will get to touch me, that he's the one who will fuck me senseless later and then hold me close while we fall asleep.

I groan, gripping at his shirt and humping against him.

"Would you feel comfortable if I tease and touch you where other people might see or even purposefully stop to watch?" he asks, and I moan.

"Yes."

"And if you get uncomfortable or if it's too much, you promise me you'll safeword?"

I nod again, happy to agree to anything if it will get us out the door and to the club. Of course, leaving this bedroom means Daddy getting off of me, which isn't exactly what I want. I whine in protest when his weight disappears. Propping myself up on my elbows, I watch as he goes to the dresser and opens the top drawer. My cock jerks, spilling a few drops of precum when I see what he pulls out.

He strides over to the bed with a bottle of lube and a small-ish plug in his hand.

"Yes," I say before he can even ask, rolling onto my belly and spreading my legs.

Daddy's hand comes down on my ass, the slightest sting making my breath catch. Okay, so maybe Sterling has a point about the whole spanking thing. I'll add spanking to my list. Except...do I *have* to be bad to get a spanking? I don't think I *want* to misbehave. Maybe I can just ask Daddy and we can do it for fun…

That's something to consider another day. Right now, I'm naked and aching while Daddy's hands are on my ass. I tilt my hips, offering up more of my ass for Kiernan to do whatever he wants with it. But instead of another spank, he kneads my ass cheeks and then parts them so I can feel the cool air on my hole.

I hear the click of the lube cap, but that's hardly enough warning before the cold, wet substance is drizzled over my hole. I gasp and recoil slightly on instinct.

"Sorry," Kiernan murmurs, using two fingers to rub the lube around, warming it in the process as he circles the outside of my pucker and then pushes inside. My balls tighten as he fucks me slowly, stroking those two fingers in and out until I'm aching for more.

"P-p-p-please," I pant.

"Later, beautiful," he says near my ear, leaning over me and pressing his lips against the side of my neck before easing his fingers out again. I barely have time to complain before he's replacing them with the plug, fucking it in and out a few times as well before slipping it into place, resting against my prostate. My cock pulses, slicking the no-doubt expensive sheets with more precum. "Now you're ready."

Daddy rolls me over onto my back and hovers over me again. I thrust up, my eyes rolling back when the plug pegs my prostate, and my hole throbs pleasantly with the fullness of the toy.

"Time to get dressed." He kisses the tip of my nose and gives me a lazy, relaxed smile like he didn't just tease the ever-living fuck out of me.

"Daddy," I complain, but he doesn't take any sympathy on me, sitting back and grabbing the shorts to hand to me.

The plug jostles inside me with every move I make to wiggle into the tight shorts, the leather sticking to my skin as I struggle to pull them up my legs. My cock bounces against my stomach and drips. A low, needy moan slips from my lips when I lift my hips up to get the shorts over my ass.

"Careful," Daddy says, helping to tuck my erection into the shorts and then zipping them for me, mindful not to catch the skin of my cock in the metal teeth. "Sit up."

I do as he says, and he helps me with the harness, buckling it so it fits snuggly but not too tight. When I'm dressed, he runs his big, strong hands over my body and makes a rumbly, humming sound.

"So damn sexy," he murmurs, grabbing

both of my ass cheeks and hauling me off the bed and into his arms for a kiss. "We're missing one thing though." He releases me, setting me on my feet, and steps into the bathroom while I wait. He returns a few seconds later with a small tube in his hand. "Pucker your lips."

I obey, feeling utterly calm in spite of my aching arousal. Every ounce of nerves I had about going tonight have vanished. I tilt my head up and purse my lips for him. The stuff he puts on feels wetter and stickier than the lipstick Nolan gave me, but it also tastes like cherries, so I'm not complaining.

"Perfect," he declares, but then he frowns and looks me over one more time. "Almost perfect." Daddy taps his chin and then smiles, striding over to the bedside table and pulling out the leather cuffs he used on me the first morning we spent in his bed together. It's hard to believe that was less than a month ago. It's hard to believe a world ever existed where I didn't belong to Kiernan.

I hold my wrists out obediently, and he fastens each one into place, leaving them a bit looser than he does when we play.

"Thank you," I say, feeling even more grounded with the cuffs around my wrists to show I belong to Daddy.

"Always," he promises before giving me

another wicked smile and hooking one finger in the front of my harness. "Let's go." He tugs, and I stumble after him, moaning happily.

Kiernan

It's been ages since I've bothered to stop by Ball and Chain. In fact, before Emerson gave me his list, I'd been considering letting my membership lapse. I glance over at my boy, dressed to sinful perfection in the passenger seat, trying his damndest not to wiggle too much, even though I can tell he's *thoroughly* enjoying the plug in that pretty little ass of his. His leather shorts are tight enough that I can see the full outline of his still-hard cock each time I glance over at him.

"I should warn you," I say as I pull into the parking lot of the club, nerves filling me as a thousand not-entirely-pleasant memories assault me. "I've played with quite a few boys who are regulars here, and some of them aren't the nicest people."

Emerson scrunches his eyebrows together and tilts his head. "Why did you like them then?"

"I'm not sure I *liked* them. I just…" I pull into a parking spot and stop the car, gripping the steering wheel as I try to sort through an answer to his question. Why *did* I play with boys I knew were greedy and selfish and ultimately not at all interested in me? "I didn't know perfect boys like you existed."

The confession lifts a weight off of me. Emerson's sweet laughter doesn't hurt either. I look over at him with a lopsided grin.

"S-s-such a charmer, Daddy."

"Just being honest, sweetheart." I lean over and kiss his cheek, not wanting to mess up his pretty pink lip gloss...*yet*. "Let's go inside."

He nods and hurries out of the car. I step out as well, unbuttoning several buttons on my shirt so my harness is visible underneath, and then I round the car and take my boy's hand.

I get a few surprised looks as we enter Ball and Chain. I really *have* been away for a while. Not that much has changed in my absence. I spot several familiar faces: Doms and subs who have been regulars even longer than I've been coming and plenty of new patrons as well.

"W-w-w-wow," Emerson whispers, moving close enough to me that he's pressed up against my side as we make our way inside. His breath catches, and I follow his gaze to a large man in a puppy hood and harness and nothing else from what I can see.

"He's a puppy," I explain, nodding to the much smaller man holding a leash beside him.

"It looks like that's his master."

"So cool."

I'm a little envious of my boy, seeing this place for the first time. I can still remember the incredibly freeing feeling of stepping inside a kink club for the first time and realizing that I wasn't a freak, or if I was, I was certainly not the only one. No one was here to judge; we're all just here to be our full selves in a way we can't be outside these doors.

"Do you want to have a seat and take things in for a few minutes, or would you like to check out some of the demonstration rooms?" I ask. He keeps looking around for a moment, seeming unable to decide, so I do what Daddies do and make a choice for him. "Go sit there." I point at an empty booth a few feet away. "I'm going to get us both some water, and I'll be right there."

He nods and does as I say. I grin with pride at the appreciative looks he gets from several people. He may not have a collar—*yet*—but the cuffs are enough of a signal to anyone who might be interested that he's already taken. I head up to the bar, which actually only serves non-alcoholic beverages for safety reasons. While I wait in line, I keep one eye on Emerson. It doesn't take long before he notices the attention he's getting and starts to preen a little. I grin at the way he sits up straighter and wiggles a little in his seat. I'd be willing to bet that he's thinking about what I might do to him in front of these people later and is getting harder and harder in those tight, leather shorts. Every few seconds, he glances in my direction as if he's reassuring himself that I'm still there, keeping an eye on him. Always, Brave Boy, *always*.

Once I get a couple of bottled waters, I join him at the table, melting inside at the impossibly bright smile he gives me as soon as I sit down.

"P-p-people keep l-l-ll-looking at me, Daddy," he says quietly, scooting close. His voice is shy, but I can see pride dancing in his eyes.

"That's because they're all wishing they were the ones to put these cuffs and harness on you, beautiful boy." I grab the front of his harness again, my cock hardening at the little gasp he lets out. I press my lips to his, hard and hungry, more than happy to have the lip gloss I put on him rub off on my own mouth. Another show of the claim I have on him, the claim we have on each other.

A throat clears next to the table, and I break the kiss to see who would dare to interrupt. I scowl when I see it's Rhett, a boy I've not only played with from time to time but one who has made his way through our little group of friends and also fucked with Sterling at a gala last year.

"So sorry to interrupt," he says with feigned sweetness.

"Are you now?" I drawl, putting an arm over the back of the booth so Emerson can scoot closer. "What can I do for you?"

"I haven't seen you around here for a while, and I couldn't believe my eyes, that's all," he says, his eyes darting between Emerson and me. "You know, if you're ever looking to play again, I'm *always* available."

I open my mouth to tell him I'm all set, but before I can, Emerson makes an adorable little growling noise and climbs onto my lap. "He's n-n-not interested."

Rhett raises both perfectly plucked eyebrows, and I swear he's about to say something snotty, but either he has more sense than I thought, or he knows a lost cause when he sees it because he simply snorts before shaking his head and walking away.

Emerson huffs in his direction like an angry little dog who doesn't want to share his owner. Good news for him: I have no interest in being shared. I lift my boy in my arms and manhandle him into a more comfortable position so he's straddling my lap.

"Down boy," I tease, carding my fingers through his hair and grinning at the grumpy look he tosses one last time over his shoulder in Rhett's general direction.

"He n-n-needs to get his own Daddy; you're mm-mine."

"Damn right, I am," I agree, running my hands down his back and resting them on his tempting ass. His annoyance melts away in an instant, replaced by a sweet, dirty smile.

"Show everyone I'm yours," he says, a slight edge of begging in his voice as he hooks his fingers around the edges of my harness and squirms in my lap.

"You want everyone to know that you're all mine?" I ask, dropping my voice low and husky as I pop the button on his pants. His cock springs free, but that's not what I'm looking for right now. Returning both hands to his ass, I pull him in for a slow, tongue-heavy kiss while I knead both cheeks greedily.

I hear the murmur of conversation as a few people stop to enjoy the admittedly tame show before moving on to more interesting things. Emerson hum and pants into my mouth, thrusting and grinding against me. I slip one hand down the back of his shorts, and he spreads his legs wider without any prompting, giving me enough room to drag my fingers through the crease between his cheeks and over the hard base of the plug resting snuggly against his hole. I could've given him a thicker plug, I know he can take it, but if I'd done that, I couldn't have played the way I have in mind for tonight.

I tease my fingers around the edge of the toy, kissing him deeper while I stroke the soft, slicked rim of his hole, jostling the plug at the same time. Emerson's moans vibrate around my tongue, his precum soaking through my shirt, causing it to stick to my stomach.

I break the kiss and ease my finger into his hole, right alongside the plug. My boy whimpers, his eyelids fluttering closed.

"Look at me," I say firmly, and he forces them open, trembling from head to toe as I start to fuck my finger in and out, stretching his hole and nudging the plug against his prostate over and over. "Dirty boy," I rumble quietly, glancing over his shoulder to see a couple of men watching with interest from a respectful distance. "Everyone can see what a slut you are for my fingers in your ass."

"*Ooh.*" He practically convulses, his cock jerking hard between us. "Don't come yet. I'm saving this for later." I wrap my fingers around the base of his cock and give him one slow stroke. Emerson breathes harder, his cheeks turning a pretty, rosy shade. "Once I'm done showing everyone here what a horny boy you are, I'm going to take you home and ride this cock for the rest of the night."

"Daddy," he gasps, bucking in my grasp. His cock pulses in my hand, spilling more thick, stringy precum down his shaft and over my knuckles.

"I'm not sure if once will be enough. I may have to cuff you to the bed and use you over and over until I'm finally satisfied," I purr next to his ear, nipping at his lobe and locking eyes with one particularly jealous Dom a few feet away who shamelessly has his hand down his pants while he watches us play. I add a second finger, the fit getting a bit tight with the help of the plug. I added enough lube earlier that it squelches sloppily with each thrust of my fingers in and out of his soft, needy hole.

"P-p-p-please." He's tugging at my harness, his knuckles brushing my sensitive nipples, and desperately mouthing at my throat without actually kissing.

"You wanted a date at the club. I can't bring you here and then take you home within half an hour," I reason, doing my best to keep the teasing out of my tone. Emerson whines helplessly, reaching the point where he's beyond words. I nip at his bottom lip and thrust my fingers inside of him again. "No more talking now unless it's your safeword."

His breath catches, his eyes going a bit

foggy as he lets himself sink into that perfectly submissive place he trusts me to give him. He manages to give a jerky nod.

"Good boy," I praise, easing my fingers out and using them to tug at his rim, sending little ripples through his body, his muscles tensing and relaxing, his cock flexing and leaking. "Now, I want to enjoy the club a while. Why don't we go see if there's a demonstration or a scene for us to enjoy?"

I make sure the plug is nestled into place and then slip my hand out of his shorts. Emerson reaches for his cock with shaking hands, but I stop him before he can tuck himself away. "I'm going to keep you like this so everyone can see what a horny boy you are."

He blinks at me a few times, his cheeks pinking again. "Snap if it's too much." Maybe I'm pushing him too far for his first time truly experimenting with exhibitionism. He doesn't snap and doesn't safeword, just humps his hard cock against me again and then looks over his shoulder to see who's watching. My sweet, dirty boy.

I help him to his feet, his cock swinging between his legs through the unzipped front of his shorts. From the corner of the room, I catch Rhett watching with a sour look on his face. There's something sad about his expression under the anger, and I'm soft enough to hope that he finds someone who can take him in hand and teach him the manners he's sorely lacking. The bratty boy isn't my problem though, so I focus on the one who is, wrapping an arm around Emerson's shoulders and leading him toward the hallway with all of the scene rooms.

We find a Shibari demonstration about to start and grab a couple of seats to watch from. The work is absolutely beautiful, as is the expression on the sub's faces when they're suspended from the ceiling. I keep my own boy on edge by reaching over and stroking his cock every time I see it starting to soften at all. The man seated next to us makes an appreciative noise every time I do it, which keeps Emerson squirming in his chair as well.

Edging my boy is a hell of a lot of fun, but it has the unfortunate side effect of keeping me on edge as well. The downside of leather is there isn't any give when my cock starts to thicken and stiffen. When the Shibari demonstration concludes, I help Emerson to his feet again and reach down to tuck him back into his shorts.

"Time to go home," I explain when he gives me a curious look.

Heat flashes through his eyes, and he moans, nodding his head rapidly.

We barely make it into the house before

Emerson is climbing up my body, making the most desperately horny sounds I've heard in my life. I help him by putting my hands under his ass and heaving him into my arms. I have enough wherewithal to kick the door closed behind me before carrying my boy down the hall to my bedroom.

My cock is achingly hard, my hole fluttering impatiently. I took the time to prep and stretch myself earlier, and I'm damn glad I did because any semblance of restraint I had was left back at the club.

When I reach the bedroom, I set my boy down on the bed and then kick off my shoes and make quick work of my pants. I groan in relief when my cock is set free, swaying between my thighs. Emerson stays put like a good boy, licking his lips and looking up at me from the bed. I grab the same lube I used earlier to put the plug in him and hastily lube myself up before peeling his own shorts off and crawling on top of him.

As soon as I'm close enough, he arches up and starts kissing my chest, drawing a shuddering breath from me when his soft, lip gloss sticky lips land on my nipple. "Harder," I grunt, putting a hand on the back of his head to encourage him. Emerson looks up at me cautiously before grazing his teeth over the same nipple. "Fuck," I sigh, the feeling going straight to my cock.

I reach between his legs and flick on the vibrations for the plug he still has seated right against his prostate. He jolts like he's being electrocuted and frantically humps up against me, turning his attention to my other nipple and biting a little harder this time.

"Fuck, sweetheart. You're driving Daddy crazy," I groan, getting into position so I can line his cock up with my hole.

He grabs onto my harness and jerks his hips, making the fat head of his cock slide against my lubed hole, catching on the rim and sending another bolt of pleasure through me. "Settle," I say firmly, getting my fingers wrapped around his base and lining him up again.

He practically vibrates with the effort to hold still but manages it like the good boy he is. The delicious sting of being stretched wide settles in the pit of my stomach as I ease myself down on his length. Emerson fists the sheets and makes wild, frenzied sounds but continues to stay nice and still for me.

It doesn't take long for me to find the perfect rhythm, bouncing up and down on his cock. My hard, heavy erection slaps against my stomach with every thrust. My thighs tremble, and my balls constrict as I ride my boy furiously, getting lost in the fullness and the feeling of his petite body under mine. Emerson kisses and nips at every inch of my skin he can reach, otherwise lying completely at my mercy as I use him as my own personal dildo, clearly loving every second of it.

The sounds he's making become increasingly frantic, his cock swelling inside me.

"Stroke me," I grunt. He manages to pry one hand off of the bed sheets and wrap it around my cock, the simple touch sending a tidal wave of sensation through me. I fuck myself harder on his cock, thrusting into his fist with each upward motion.

With a loud growl, my inner muscles clench around him, and my cock starts to pulse in his hand, covering us both in my hot, sticky cum. Emerson lets out a wild wail, the heat of his release filling me, the throbbing of his cock answering mine as I continue to ride him, taking him over and over even as my thighs grow tired, and my orgasm starts to fade.

I have just enough energy to roll off of him, turn off his plug, and pull my boy into my arms.

"Was the club everything you hoped?" I ask once I catch my breath.

"Better," he murmurs sleepily, nuzzling his face into my chest. I need to take both of our harnesses off and take his plug out, but that can wait a few minutes. I wrap my arms around him and stroke a hand up and down the curve of his spine.

I knew my bed felt empty before Emerson came along, but I underestimated just how full he would actually make it feel in all the best ways. Not just my bed: my life, my heart, everything. I slide my hand up to his neck, his noticeably bare neck.

"How would you feel about a collar, Brave Boy?" I ask delicately.

He tilts his head back and looks up at me with a searching expression. "Isn't that r-r-r-really serious?"

I nod. "I'm feeling pretty serious about you. But if you're not ready or a collar doesn't appeal, I won't be offended."

A slow smile creeps over his lips. "As l-l-long as it's not diamond," he bargains, and I chuckle.

"Deal." I dip down for a soft, sweet kiss, memorizing the shape of his lips again, never seeming to tire of it.

If I ask him to move in too, would that be pushing it? Maybe just one serious proposal at a time...

CHAPTER 20

Emerson

I hate spreadsheets. Or, more accurately, they hate me. I groan and drop my head to the desk. Why didn't anyone tell me that owning a business would involve so much math and bookkeeping? Maybe I should just hire an accountant. I can certainly afford it, and it will save me a hell of a lot of headaches.

A light tap on my door draws my attention away from the torture of balancing the books. I left Sterling to watch the store for a while, and I'm assuming he has a question about a shipment or something.

"C-c-come in," I call, a smile jumping to my lips when I see Kiernan step through the door instead of Sterling. "Daddy."

"Hi, sweetheart. I brought lunch." He holds up a takeout bag, and my stomach growls right on cue.

Daddy frowns. "Sounds like I got here just in time."

I smile and close my laptop, shuffling my stack of paperwork messily off to the side to clear the space for us to eat. Kiernan's eyes linger on the top sheet of paper for a second before he studiously looks away, focusing on pulling the takeout containers out of the bag.

I glance at the paper to see what caught his interest, and I realize it's the bank statement I had printed out. It's not something I'm trying to keep a secret necessarily; money just hasn't exactly come up between us. Obviously, Kiernan is rich as fuck, much richer than I am. But I'm not hurting either.

"Mm-my grandpa left me s-s-some money," I explain, and he nods. "And...I had some mm-m-money of my own." More important than the number of zeros in my bank account is how I got them. I don't make it a habit of talking about my writing. In fact, I've never told anyone. Not because I'm embarrassed or ashamed of what I write, but because then they might ask questions that I don't care to answer. I don't have anything to hide from Daddy though. He *should* know about my writing.

"You don't have to explain. It's good for me to know that financial help isn't something you need from me, but we can leave it at that," he assures me.

"I w-w-want to tell you." I open the container he set in front of me and dig into the Chow Mein he brought. He doesn't rush me, simply eats his own lunch quietly while I work out the words in my head first so I can get them out. "I w-write erotica b-b-b-books."

He pauses with an egg roll halfway to his mouth, his eyebrows shooting up and a slow smile taking over his expression. "You write erotica books?" he repeats, and I nod. "Under a pen name?" He sounds almost giddy. "I wonder if I've read them."

I remember him mentioning that he enjoys gay erotica, but at the time, I thought he was only teasing, trying to get me all hot and bothered simply to see if he could. My cheeks heat. While I'm not ashamed to write erotica, I *am* a little embarrassed by the cheesy erotica pen name I chose. "Dick Stroker," I mutter quickly before stuffing my mouth full of some food.

"*You're* Dick Stroker? I'm dating Dick Stroker?"

I duck my head and try to hide my grin. I guess he has heard of me. I *do* have a bit of a following, I suppose.

"It s-s-started for fun." I shrug like it's no big deal, even if it has been something I've put an excessive amount of energy into for almost a decade now.

"You're the biggest name in gay erotica. Your books are always at the top of the charts," he says. My cheeks get even hotter, and I shrug again. "You're full of surprises, aren't you?"

Kiernan

It takes me the rest of lunch to process the new information that Em has given me. Not only does he have a substantial amount of money in the bank—side note, we're going to have to discuss that rust bucket of a car he's been driving and the state of his furniture—but more importantly, he's my favorite author.

I thought I couldn't be more impressed and enamored with the boy, but clearly, he's out to prove me wrong. And I'm happy to let him do so.

When we're both finished eating, I clean up the containers and then round the desk, picking my boy up out of his chair and then sitting down with him on my lap.

"Hi, Daddy," he says with a laugh, resting his head on my shoulder as I wrap my arms around him.

"Hello, sweetheart." I kiss his cheek. "Read me something."

Emerson's eyes go wide, and he gives a quick shake of his head. "I c-can't."

"Sure, you can. Your stutter doesn't put me off. I thought you'd have realized that by now." I gently stroke my fingers up and down his spine.

He tugs his bottom lip between his teeth and worries it. "I d-d-don't usually stutter as much when I read," he admits. "I've thought about d-d-doing open mic n-n-nights here even."

"Perfect. Read to me."

"It's embarrassing." Emerson buries his face in the crook of my neck, and I smile, always happy to have my boy close.

"Be brave for me," I encourage. He whines but wiggles around and opens his laptop. "Good boy." I kiss the back of his neck.

I wait patiently while he clicks around for a moment, pulling up a Word doc he seems to have been recently working on and scrolling a bit. He takes a deep breath and starts to read.

"H-H-his pretty lips smirk up at me, inches away from the fat head of my cock, a glistening pearl of precum at my slit, threatening to spill over and trickle down my shaft, firm and clutched in his hand.

His eyes flicker to the building across the way again, his eyelids drooping to half-lidded. Anderson l-l-licks his lips, his breath fanning over my cock, throbbing hard and painful. His tongue darts out to wet his lips, and my hips twitch, urging me to grab his cheeks, force him to part those pretty lips, and fuck his mouth until it's dripping with my cum.

"Do you think anyone can see us out here?" he asks breathlessly. My first instinct is to reassure him we'll be fine, no one will see. But the hint of excitement in his eyes tells me that's not what he wants to hear.

I shouldn't be surprised that his current work in progress has an exhibitionism kink. In fact, now that I'm thinking about all of the Dick Stroker books I've read, there are more than a few with public and semi-public sex. I know he gave me a list of his fantasies, but it wouldn't hurt to brush up on the books again as well. While he reads, I slip my hand into his pants and tease his soft cock with my fingertips until it starts to swell and stiffen.

Emerson squirms and stops reading.

"Keep going," I command, wrapping my hand fully around his growing erection and stroking him slowly.

"MMM-M-maybe. It'd be easy enough for someone to look out of their window across the street, only one floor up. They might not even be trying to watch, not at first. They might be horrified, and then a little curious..." His breath hitches, and

he thrusts into my grip.

"What's going to happen? Is someone watching?" I prompt, and Emerson nods. "Keep reading," I whisper near his ear.

"Anderson mm-m-moans, and his mmm-mouth wraps around my cock..." I drag my thumb over the head of his cock, drawing another whine from his throat. "Daddy," Emerson gasps.

"Focus, baby, there's a blowjob happening here." I nip playfully at his earlobe and gently pinch the tip of his cock, making my boy wail. "Someone's going to hear you if you keep that up."

Emerson's cock jerks in my grasp, his whole body trembling, but my boy pulls through and keeps reading like he's supposed to.

"His tongue caresses the thickly veined underside of my sh-sh-sh-shaft, coaxing a shiver out of me, while his l-l-lll-lips suction around me, the heat of his throat slowly engulfing me."

"Mm," I hum, sucking the side of his throat and stroking him faster. "Sounds like Anderson is a good little cock sucker, isn't he?"

My boy nods rapidly, squirming and thrusting into my grip.

"Oh fuck, Anderson," I mm-m-moan. My eyes drift up, my head tilting back, and a motion catches my eye. Someone at their window, just like I was

teasing. Someone's actually up there, watching us.

His cock swells, and a cascade of precum trickles over my knuckles. "Come for Daddy," I murmur near his ear, and that's all it takes for Emerson to let loose. He drops his head back against my shoulder and fucks into my fist, once, twice, and then he's pulsing and trembling, filling my hand with his hot, sticky cum.

"Daddy, Daddy, Daddy," he chants over and over, turning his head toward me so I can nibble and kiss his lips as his orgasm starts to fade.

"I love you." The words are past my lips before I have a chance to consider them. His eyes fly open, the relaxed, orgasm-drunk look gone in an instant.

"You...?" He scrunches his eyebrows together, his forehead wrinkling and a frown marring his pretty lips.

Maybe this isn't the exact right moment to tell him, with my hand down his pants, his cock softening in my cum-drenched grip, but fuck it, my heart is so full of love for this boy that I can't stop myself from saying it again.

"I love you."

He blinks at me, his cheeks pink and his chest still rising and falling rapidly, whether from his orgasm or the shock, I'm not sure. Maybe it's both. A dozen different emotions pass over his face, and I wonder if maybe I've broken his brain.

"I..."

"It's okay." I kiss him gently one more time. "I didn't say it to pressure you to say it back. I needed you to know, and now you do. Process, breathe, and we'll talk later."

Emerson nods slowly, letting me slip my hand out of his pants without protest and lift him off my lap. I use the bathroom off his office to wash up and then kiss him one more time before taking off with one last promise that we'll talk later.

Maybe it was too fast. Maybe I've terrified the poor boy. But I don't think it's anything a little time to breathe won't fix. Tonight, I'll pick him up and take him home to sleep in my bed where he belongs, and he'll tell me how he feels when he's ready. I'm nothing if not patient.

CHAPTER 21

Emerson

Kiernan is in love with me. I've been trying to wrap my head around it since he dropped those words on me like a bomb yesterday and left me completely speechless. After he left the shop, I ended up texting him to tell him that I needed some alone time to process rather than going to his place. There's no doubt in my mind I'm completely and utterly in love with him. But I'm glad he gave me the chance to take a breath and find my words so I'll be able to say it back without stumbling through it.

I text him from his driveway with a grin on my lips and a flutter in my stomach.

Emerson: Come outside, Daddy

It takes a minute or two before he sees my message.

Daddy: Is everything okay?

Emerson: Of course. Just come outside.

I should've guessed that he wouldn't believe me that everything is fine. It takes less than a second for Kiernan to come flying out the front door like he's sure I'm going to be on fire on his front lawn. His eyes land on my car as he sprints down the stairs in a half-buttoned shirt and no shoes.

I roll down my window and shake my head at him. "I told you I'm okay."

"I didn't expect you this morning." He looks me over like he's trying to make extra sure that I really am intact and safe. Once he's satisfied, he returns my smile, leaning down and resting his hands on my window. I pucker my lips for a kiss, and he gives it to me because he's Daddy and he always gives me what I need.

"G-g-go put your shoes on," I say, earning an arched eyebrow for my bossy tone. "P-please, Daddy?"

"Do you want to come in?" he asks, and I shake my head.

"G-g-get shoes, then I have a d-date planned."

With one last amused look in my direction, he jogs back up the steps and disappears into the house. It doesn't take long before he returns, this time fully dressed and wearing shoes, as requested. He makes his way around to the passenger seat and gets into the car.

"Where are we off to?" he asks, and I just smirk at him. I'm not about to spoil the surprise. I just hope he likes it. It's not anything fancy like he's used to.

I do my best not to bounce in my seat or get distracted by the mountain of sexy that is Daddy in the seat next to me. I want to blurt out how much I love him, how lucky I am to have met him, and how I hope I get to be his boy forever and ever. But I also want to be able to kiss him and climb onto his lap when I say it, so probably best to wait until I'm not driving.

Kiernan looks surprised when I pull into the parking lot of a little park with a cute oasis of trees and a small pond. It's man-made and maintained, obviously. Either way, there are ducks, which is clearly the important part.

I get out of the car, and Daddy does the same, following me around to the trunk, which I pop open to pull out the picnic basket I packed as well as a blanket and a bag of birdseed. I barely have all of my items gathered into my arms before he swoops in and takes them for me, jerking his chin toward the park.

"Lead the way; I've got all this."

I pick out a nice, shady spot under a tree near the pond, and he lays down the blanket while I start to unpack the food. I went full breakfast mode with pancakes, fruit, eggs, and bacon. I even brought stuff for mimosas.

We get settled and both dig into the food. My heart beats fast, and I keep shooting him sweet, nervous smiles as I try to work up the courage to say the words I spent half the night practicing aloud so I'd get them right.

"Strawberry for your thoughts?" he asks, holding out a piece of fruit for me. I lean forward and pluck it from between his fingers with my teeth, licking the juices from my lips and chewing it slowly.

"I'm th-th-thinking about w-w-what you said yesterday."

Worry crosses his expression. "I don't want you to feel pressured, Brave Boy."

"N-no one has said it to me before," I confess. I know my grandpa loved me, but he wasn't the overly expressive type. My mom was too busy not giving a shit that I existed, and compared to my dad, she was parent of the year. So here I am, trying to work up the courage to say the words for the first time to the most perfect, caring, amazing Daddy I ever could've asked for.

"Oh, sweetheart." He reaches for me and

pulls me into his arms. I press my face into the crook of his neck, breathing deep to pull his scent into my lungs. "You are incredible and so worthy of love."

I nod and sniffle, realizing for the first time that my cheeks are damp…that I'm crying. I dash away the tears with the back of my hand and lean back, tilting my head to look at Kiernan.

"I love you," I say as confidently and clearly as I've said anything in my life.

The smile that lights up his face is all the assurance I need that he loves me back just as fiercely. Of course he's generous enough to give me the words too.

"I love you," Daddy murmurs, kissing my cheeks, the tip of my nose, and finally my lips.

We finish our breakfast picnic just like that, with me on Daddy's lap, laughing together while we hand feed each other bits of the food I packed and tossing birdseed to the ducks in between bites.

It's the absolute definition of perfection. Just like Daddy is.

Kiernan

My heart is still singing from Emerson's declaration of love as we pack up the empty food containers and fold the blanket back up. It's too lovely of a day to head straight home, so once we've put everything back into his trunk, I grab my boy's hand and we decide to go for a walk to explore a bit.

We stumble on a rummage sale, and Emerson excitedly starts to sift through boxes of dusty items, pausing to sneeze every so often in a ridiculously adorable way. I join him, picking another box and looking through it, glancing up every so often simply to enjoy the look of pure joy on my boy's face as he fills his arms with what appears to be useless junk. If the junk makes him happy though, who am I to complain?

There isn't much of interest in any of the boxes until I stumble on one filled with old books. I look over to find Emerson sniffing a candle a few feet away, and then I return my attention to the box. Most of the books have seen better days, falling apart from the binding, the pages stained from age. When I reach the bottom of the box, I find one that appears to be in surprisingly good condition. My heart leaps as I realize what it is—a first edition of *Alice in Wonderland*.

I pull it out carefully and ease it open. The binding is still intact, all of the pages in place.

The musty smell of old books hits me, but I know for some people that's half the appeal.

"Excuse me, how much is this?" I ask the woman who seems to be the owner of all this junk.

"All the books are two dollars."

"Hmm." I frown, reaching into my pocket to pull out my wallet. All I have are hundred-dollar bills on me, so I hand her one and tuck the book under my arm.

"I don't have change for this much."

"Keep it," I say easily, too excited to show Emerson what I found for him to worry about it. I understand now about the watch I gave him. I picked it because I thought it would show how much I cared because it was expensive. But this book, a first edition of his favorite book from childhood, is a gift that actually means something to him. That's what a gift *should* be. Such a simple lesson, you'd think I'd have learned it prior to the age of forty.

"W-w-what did you find?" he asks, and I hand him the book. Emerson gasps, his eyes going wide as he gently takes it from me like it's made of glass. "This is amazing. Thank you." He pets the cover reverently, and my heart swells.

"Anything," I promise, pulling him into my arms and kissing him senseless.

We pull up into my driveway a few hours later and Emerson puts his car into park. I unbuckle my seatbelt but don't make a move to get out. In light of our conversation earlier, the question that's been lingering on my mind for over a week now shouldn't be all that difficult to ask. My heart beats too fast anyway as I turn to my boy.

"Do you like your apartment?" I ask as casually as I can manage.

"It's fine." He shrugs and cocks his head like he's trying to figure out what I'm getting at.

"Okay, but does it have an infinity pool?" I challenge, quirking an eyebrow.

I see the exact moment my meaning sinks in. He smiles and then hurries to cover it up with a look of feigned indifference. "A p-p-pool? Is that all you h-have to offer?"

"Hmm." I stroke my beard and consider the challenge. "If a pool doesn't do it for you, how about Daddy's attention on command, being read to sleep every night, and as many vibrating butt plugs as you can carry?"

Emerson barks out a laugh. "Okay," he answers.

"Okay? You'll move in with me?"

He nods, and for a few moments, we just

stare at each other, beyond needing any words as we simply exist in this moment until I can't resist his lips a second longer. I lean over the center console and claim his lips, kissing him slowly and sweetly, on and on until I'm not even positive we're two separate people anymore rather than one perfect entity.

"I love you," I murmur against his lips. It's a travesty he's never heard the words before. Luckily, I have an entire lifetime to rectify the injustice.

"I love you," he whispers back, sending my heart into overdrive. I can't wait to have my boy under my roof. Soon, he'll have my collar and, one day, a ring—all symbols that he's mine, but the most important thing is that he knows it. He's mine, and I'm his. Always.

CHAPTER 22

Kiernan

I can't imagine a better feeling than stepping into the house at the end of a long day and seeing signs of my boy everywhere. He moved in a little over a week ago, and his things are already scattered everywhere: his shoes laying haphazard near the door, books everywhere as if he can't bear the thought of not having one to pick up at a moment's notice to read. I suggested an e-reader for him and received an exceptionally affronted look in response. Apparently, the smell and weight of a book is an important part of his reading experience. Who am I to argue with what makes my boy happy?

We have plans to have our friends over later for dinner to celebrate our new cohabitation, but first, there's something I've been working up the nerve to do for days now...

I remove my shoes and loosen my tie, and then go in search of Emerson. It's easy enough to find him by following the sound of off-key singing—A Taylor Swift song, naturally. I lean against the closet door for a moment before he notices I'm there, enjoying the sight of him naked and shaking his ass while he hangs up his clothes in the empty spot I made for him.

I expect him to stop singing when he notices he's not alone, but instead, when his eyes land on me, he grins and sings louder. I join in on the chorus, stepping into the closet and pulling him into my arms to dance with him. He laughs and follows my lead, waltzing around the space, his body pressed against mine in the most perfect of ways. The blush on his cheeks and the smile on his lips are far beyond the most beautiful sight I've ever seen.

"I have something for you," I say, falling in love all over again at the way Emerson's face lights up instantly and then morphs into a mildly cautious expression. He's worried it's more diamonds. Adorable. "Be a good boy and go get on the bed." I release him and give him a gentle pat on the ass as encouragement.

He makes a cute little sound, full of excitement as he slips past me to get out of the large closet and goes straight to the bed, settling himself in the center with his legs crossed and his hands folded. Such a good boy. A deep sense of satisfaction settles in my chest. Not just satisfaction: adoration, joy, so much love I can barely breathe.

My nerves start to prickle as I cross the room and pull open the second drawer on my dresser. Obviously, I was smart enough to skip the diamonds when I was having it designed, but I'm still anxious about whether my boy will like it. I decided to go simple and elegant. Emerson is already beautiful enough on his own, the last thing he needs is showy accessories.

My hands are nearly shaking as I pull out the slim box and carry it over to the bed. He cranes his neck to try to get a glimpse of what's in my hands, practically vibrating with impatience. I smile and stop at the foot of the bed, taking a second to admire my beautiful, perfect boy, completely bare for me as per his rules. Since moving in, I've been able to better enforce his bedtime rule, and the exhaustion is all but gone from his features, his skin more vibrant now, and the circles under his eyes little more than a distant memory.

I reach out with one hand and stroke his cheek, dragging my fingers along his jaw and then down to the base of his throat, where I let them linger for a moment before handing him the box.

"Daddy?" he asks, sounding slightly breathless.

"Open it," I say with more confidence than I feel, holding my breath as he obeys. I keep an eye on his expression as he works the lid off and peers inside at the custom-made leather collar. I had it made with a deep purple dye, a sparkly unicorn charm hanging from the tag loop.

"Daddy," he breathes again, this time his voice full of awe as he reaches into the box and pulls out the collar.

"It's the collar we talked about. If you prefer to wear it only to the club and at home, that's okay, or you can keep it on all the time. But this way you have a reminder all the time that you're mine and I'm yours."

He nods rapidly, a few stray tears rolling down his cheeks as he runs his fingers all over the soft, smooth leather. It only takes him a second to find the engraving on the inside. "Brave Boy," he murmurs, feeling along the sunken letters with his fingers.

"I thought that would be a good reminder of who you are, sweetheart."

He shakes his head. "Who I w-want to be."

"Who you are," I insist, beckoning him forward with the crook of my finger. He inches closer, and I take the collar from him. "Chin up."

Emerson does as I say, tilting his head up to give me the best access to his neck, and I put the collar on him, slipping my fingers underneath it to check that it's not too tight. Another wave of satisfaction rolls through me, seeing my boy wearing nothing but my collar.

His hands go to it, and his smile widens. "I'm n-never taking it off."

"Okay," I agree, hooking my fingers into the collar and using it to tug him closer. He moans, and his cock hardens, his eyelids fluttering closed as the most enchanting look of peace washes over his face. I claim his lips with my own, kissing him deeply, owning every inch of his mouth just like he owns every inch of me, inside and out.

Emerson

I could kiss Daddy all day long. His lips on mine feel even more perfect with the weight of the collar around my neck, the warm, soft leather caressing my skin. My cock was already hard before he kissed me, but as his tongue moves against mine, I pant and squirm, aching all over for his touch.

"Our friends will be here in a few minutes," he reminds me, and I groan unhappily. Not that I don't want to see our friends, but I'd much prefer an orgasm first. Kiernan kisses me for another minute, his tongue stroking leisurely over mine, his lips caressing mine, and his hands teasing my body. I grumble when he breaks the kiss and lifts me off the bed, setting me on my feet. "Get dressed."

I huff but do as he says, returning to the closet to pick out some clothes to wear. With a playful grin, I grab my favorite unicorn shirt and tug it on, followed by a pair of jeans, not bothering with underwear. When I step back out into the bedroom, Daddy looks me over with a heated expression.

"Cute shirt," he says playfully, echoing the first words he ever spoke to me the day that I stepped into that intimidating conference room alongside Sterling to pitch them the idea of investing in our mobile library idea.

I smile and cross the room to kiss him just one more time. Well, one more time for right now. There's no way I'll ever get enough of him.

Our friends arrive a short time later, and Kiernan fires up the grill on the back patio while we all get comfortable around the pool. Sterling, Nolan, and I sit on the edge of the pool with our feet dangling into the water while Barrett, Alden, and Gannon sit on the patio furniture, discussing work from the sounds of things. Boo. Boring.

It's hard to miss the looks Gannon keeps shooting at Nolan, a little bit of longing and a whole lot of heat. But they're nothing compared to the way Alden is looking at the quiet, broody man. Seems complicated if you ask me, but maybe they'll figure it out. For what it's worth, Nolan keeps shooting covert peeks at both of them.

"It's so pretty," Sterling says, eyeing my collar. "Daddy, I want a collar."

Barrett pauses his conversation and smiles at his boy. "You've got it, Pretty Boy."

Something tells me that's his answer for just about anything Sterling asks for. Not that I have any room to talk, considering how much my Daddy spoils me.

If you would've told ten-year-old me that one day I'd have not only best friends but a man who loves me so wholly I can feel it in every look and touch he gives me, I'm not sure I would've believed it. I used to lie awake at night and imagine a life like this, full of love and laughter and acceptance, but part of me never thought it would be real. Maybe that's why I fell in love with fictional worlds so fully; I thought they might be the only place true happiness existed. Now I have the real thing, and I'm never letting it go.

Kiernan strides over and lifts me up, making me laugh in surprise as he swings me into his arms and kisses me, a hard, quick peck on my lips before setting me back down.

"W-what was that for?" I ask, regaining my

balance.

"It's impossible to see you and not kiss you," he explains with an unrepentant grin.

Nolan sighs from behind me, and I turn to see him watching the two of us with a wistful expression. "Okay, so maybe a Daddy doesn't seem like the *worst* thing ever," he concedes. "Still not sure I want to follow rules though."

Sterling giggles.

"That's what spankings are for," Kiernan explains, waggling his eyebrows and drawing more laughter from all three of us.

"I l-love you, Daddy." I wrap my arms around him and press my face into his bare chest for a moment, reminding myself again that this is all real: my life, the love he has for me, all of it.

"I love you too, Brave Boy." He presses his nose to the top of my head, his hot breath tickling my scalp. "More than anything."

"Mm-more than *anything*?" I tease. "Mm-more than diamonds and fancy c-c-cars and *books*?"

"More than every breath in my lungs and every star in the sky," he answers, and I make a mental note to add that absolute swoon to my next book. Something tells me Kiernan is going to give me endless inspiration. One day we'll both be old and wrinkly, and he'll still be saying the sweetest things to me. I can totally live with that.

"Me too, Daddy." I squeeze him tighter and let myself feel all of this impossibly big love inside me. Only for Kiernan. Always for Kiernan. With Daddy at my side, I know I can be anything, especially the brave boy I've always wanted to be.

EPILOGUE

One Year Later

Emerson

"Th-th-this is a horrible idea." I pace back and forth beside the stage. Well, not exactly a stage, but a cleared area of the shop where I set up a microphone and some lighting for the open mic nights that I stupidly decided to start hosting.

"It's going to be brilliant," Kiernan insists, grabbing my wrist and tugging me closer.

I shake my head and bury my face in his broad, familiar chest. "I c-c-c-can't."

"You can," he says firmly. "Remember what I said?"

I shake my head again, even though I remember *exactly* what he said. I've thought about it a million times in the past year, holding it close whenever I feel less than brave.

"Yes, you do." Of course he sees right through me. "Anyone who would judge or make fun of you for something you can't control is saying more about themselves than they are about you." Daddy tilts my head up and presses a soft kiss to my lips. "You are fucking brilliant and beautiful and brave as all hell. You've got this."

I take a deep breath and eye the stage again. Sterling agreed to emcee the very first open mic night at Unicorn Books, and he's already standing in front of the microphone stand, waving at a few customers and fellow artists who are planning to do readings or performances tonight as well.

"W-w-w-ww-wish me l-luck."

"You don't need luck." Daddy gives me one last squeeze and then spins me around to point me toward the stage.

"Welcome, y'all," Sterling says cheerfully. "We're so happy to have everybody here for the first of many open mic nights at Unicorn Books. We've got snacks and coffee on that table over there, and we hope y'all enjoy all the talented artists we have tonight. To start the evenin' off, the owner of the shop himself, Emerson Brooks." He waves me up with an encouraging smile.

How many deep breaths can I take before I just have to take the plunge and step up into that blindingly bright spotlight? I cast one last look at Kiernan seated in the front row, giving me a thumbs up.

I had no idea when I made that M4M: Kink profile that it would change my life the way it has. Would I ever have been brave enough to tell him how I was feeling in person? I'd like to think I would. After all, he's shown me a million ways to be brave in the past year. Then again, it's easy to be brave when I know my Daddy is always there to catch me if I fall.

I mouth "I love you" in his direction and then square my shoulders and step in front of the microphone.

"H-h-h-hi, everyone." I fiddle with the paperback in my hands, already opened to the page I want, the spine creased from how many times I've read these paragraphs aloud over and over for the past few weeks in preparation for tonight. Maybe I should've picked something a little less risqué for my first public reading, then again, when have I ever done things by half? No need to start now. "I'm g-g-going to read f-f-from…" I hold up the book to show off the title. No need to waste words on something they can all see. "I w-w-wrote it…obviously." The audience chuckles, and I roll my eyes at myself, my cheeks heating. "Anyway, here w-w-w-we go."

I lick my lips and dive in. "*C-C-C-Caleb's hole was aching to be stretched and used by Dominic. He'd thought of nothing else for weeks now… mm-maybe months. Time seemed to cease to have any meaning when Dominic entered the room. He somehow managed to become the very center of Caleb's universe, and there was nothing either of them could do about it. There was nothing Caleb wanted to do about it, other than bend over and shamelessly beg the sturdy, dominant man to have his way with him.*

"S-s-s-such a pretty little slut," Dominic purred, taking Caleb's face between his large, calloused hands and stroking his cheeks with his thumbs. It was all the shy sub could do to keep from shaking. He darted his tongue out to wet his lips and nodded. He'd be happy to be Dominic's slut. He'd be happy to be Dominic's anything...or better yet, his everything."

I only stumble a few times as I fall into a rhythm, pausing when I need to in order to gather my words before continuing. Every time I look up, I see all of my friends in the front row, right beside Kiernan, all appearing riveted by my words. My confidence grows with every word out of my mouth until I finally reach the end, and the audience sits silently for a few seconds before erupting into applause. I let out a relieved breath and step away to cede the stage back to Sterling.

"Wow." He fans himself. "I think we all need a cold shower after that one."

Everyone laughs in agreement, a few people catcalling. I smile and slip into the seat next to Kiernan, who, to my surprise, stands up.

"Our next performer, well... I'll just let him explain." Sterling gestures to Kiernan.

"What are you doing?" I hiss, and my Daddy smirks at me.

"You'll see," he says with a wink before striding up to the stage. He adjusts the microphone to the right height and then smooths his hands down the front of his shirt. If I didn't know any better, I'd think he was nervous. "Hi. I'll be honest, the only talent I have isn't one you folks came to see tonight." He waggles his eyebrows, and I snort a laugh. These people should be so lucky. "No, I'm not half as talented as the sweet, incredible man I have the privilege to call mine." He looks at me, and my hand goes immediately to the soft leather collar that rests around my neck, where it's been since the day he gave it to me. "But something's been bothering me recently," he goes on, and I frown, tightening my grip on my collar. "Emerson, my brave, perfect boy..." He reaches into his pocket and drops to one knee.

My breath catches, and I jump out of my chair. "W-w-w-what are you doing?" I ask for a second time, my throat going dry. Is this for real? I'm dreaming, right? I have to be dreaming.

Kiernan pulls a small, velvety box out of his pocket and pops it open to reveal a surprisingly simple silver band. "I don't want to live another day of my life without you. You're already mine, and I'm already yours, but why don't we go ahead and make it official?"

I nod rapidly, not trusting my voice. But just in case there's any confusion, I launch myself at him, tackling him in a kiss and smiling against his lips.

"Is that a yes, sweetheart?" he checks, laughing against my mouth.

"Yes," I whisper, letting him take my hand and slip the ring into place.

The collar already meant forever to me, but the ring is nice too. Either way, I already planned to spend the rest of my life with Daddy, making each other happier and better every single day. Forever and ever. And then hopefully a little longer after that.

The End

ABOUT THE AUTHOR

K.M. Neuhold is a complete romance junkie. Pansexual and polyamorous, she often describes herself as being in love with love. She loves to write stories full of bearded, cinnamon roll men who get super swoony HEAs. Her philosophy is there's so much angst and sadness for LGBT characters in media, all she wants is to give them the happiest happily ever afters she can with little angst, tons of humor, and SO MUCH STEAM. K.M. fully admits to her tendencies of making sure every side character has a full backstory that will likely always lead to every book turning into a series or spin-off. When she's not writing she's a lion tamer, an astronaut, and a superhero...just kidding, she's likely watching Netflix and snuggling with her husky while her amazing husband brings her coffee.

Lightning Source UK Ltd.
Milton Keynes UK
UKHW012247270821
389594UK00004B/1147

9 798749 255737